"I WANT TO GO TO BED NOW—ALONE . . ."

"Oh, I'm sure of that." He let her feel his fingers against the soft skin between her breasts. An instant later, those same fingers caught her chin, lifting it so that she was forced to meet his gaze. "I wonder if you could be persuaded to change your mind?"

His voice was gentle and deep, his gaze almost mesmerizing. Despite herself, Kelsey yielded to the hard masculine arm that moved down to her hips, molding her body to his. As his head bent over hers, she relaxed in his unyielding embrace.

After all, she thought, just one kiss couldn't matter, could it. . . ?

Return Engagement

by Glenna Finley

For this is a sort of engagement, you see,
Which is binding on you, but not binding on me.

— WM. ALLEN BUTLER

A SIGNET BOOK

NEW AMERICAN LIBRARY

TIMES MIRROR

NAL BOOKS ARE AVAILABLE AT QUANTITY DIS-
COUNTS WHEN USED TO PROMOTE PRODUCTS OR
SERVICES. FOR INFORMATION, PLEASE WRITE
TO PREMIUM MARKETING DIVISION, THE NEW
AMERICAN LIBRARY, INC., 1633 BROADWAY,
NEW YORK, NEW YORK 10019.

Copyright © 1981 by Glenna Finley

SIGNET TRADEMARK REG. U.S. PAT. OFF. AND FOREIGN COUNTRIES
REGISTERED TRADEMARK—MARCA REGISTRADA
HECHO EN CHICAGO, U.S.A.

SIGNET, SIGNET CLASSICS, MENTOR, PLUME, MERIDIAN AND NAL
BOOKS are published by The New American Library, Inc.,
1633 Broadway, New York, New York 10019

First Printing, November, 1981

1 2 3 4 5 6 7 8 9

PRINTED IN THE UNITED STATES OF AMERICA

Chapter 1

KELSEY Dodge stood on the front porch of her hilltop home in Santa Fe and sternly addressed the other occupant. "This is my final warning. From now on, you stay around at night or come back at a decent hour. You might even get a steady job like the rest of us. And one more thing—stop dragging your tacky friends home with you."

A down-at-the-heels tomcat who was on the receiving end of her lecture stayed comfortably on his side but kept one paw clamped over a struggling beetle.

Kelsey bent down and lifted the paw, allowing the insect to make his escape. The tiger cat twitched his tail angrily showing that he possessed plenty of red-blooded instincts, even though he was completely lacking in blue-blooded ones.

Kelsey didn't waver under the challenge. "Meals in this house are served in the kitchen," she answered as she stood up. "In a dish—not à la carte. You might as well get used to it."

The cat turned his head to watch his quarry scuttle off and then yawned. Obviously he'd heard the dialogue before and he wasn't impressed.

"Don't take it so hard," Kelsey said dryly, and

1

then, unable to restrain herself, reached down and stroked the rough head. She was very fond of the scroungy vagrant who dropped in at her godfather's home where she'd been house-sitting for the past month. She couldn't say as much for his offerings of mice, small birds, and insects which were deposited in her bedroom at regular intervals. They were hard to get accustomed to—especially when she stumbled barefooted over them in the early morning. So far, the tomcat hadn't shown any tendency to change his habits—and Kelsey found herself surrendering to his masculine designs.

She stepped over his relaxed form and started down the gravel drive toward the mail box on the main road—a hundred feet away. Her lips tightened as she thought about masculine stubbornness in general before she determinedly relegated such unpleasant thoughts to the back of her mind.

It wasn't difficult on such an early August morning. The sun was shining brightly in the clear blue sky but it was still refreshingly cool at seven thousand feet in that northern part of New Mexico.

As always, the fresh mountain air bore traces of the juniper and piñon pine that dotted the rocky, hard-packed soil all around her. The dark green vegetation was in sharp contrast to the bleached dirt and scruffy gray chamisa undergrowth by the drive. When she'd first arrived in New Mexico, Kelsey had been surprised by the unmanicured Sante Fe real estate. Then she'd learned that while land holdings in that part of the world came in big chunks, the water supply didn't. As a result, residents did their gardening in front of the house or displayed inner patios ablaze with color.

The yard beside Kelsey was left in its natural state except for scattered bird-feeding platforms to provide interest. That morning the feeder by the drive was tenanted by three kinds of jays. Below them, at ground level, two jack rabbits happily munched on the leftovers.

The fluttering of bird wings on the wooden platform was the only sound to be heard in the still morning air. There was the customary haze over the Guadalupe Mountains to the south, but the outlines of the soaring Sangre de Cristo Mountains to the east and north were clearly defined against the vivid sky. Kelsey uttered a throaty murmur of satisfaction, feeling at that moment as if she had the top of the world to herself.

She didn't dwell on her solitude for long. From the beginning of her stay in Sante Fe, she'd learned that such thoughts could be dangerous, an occupational hazard in her temporary house-sitting job for Lucius Belmont.

Just the day before she'd learned that her godfather's stay would be extended in Brussels where he was conferring with some scientific NATO colleagues. His last letter showed that the delay in his return might jeopardize her vacation plans later in the month. What he didn't know was that her schedule had changed—a Mexican jaunt had been scuttled—so she hoped to continue her house-sitting duties for a few more weeks. After that, she'd return to Manhattan and resume her career as a scenery designer.

She was sure that her godfather would be happy to hear of her change of plans, and it merely required a long-distance phone call to tell him. As soon as she got back to the house she could place the call with the overseas operator. And once she'd settled the house situation, she'd collect the set designs she'd been working on and drive to Santa Fe to go over them with Norman.

Her expression softened as she thought about Norman Wilkens and how much his friendship had meant over the past months. If her feminine ego hadn't been at such a low ebb, probably she wouldn't have given a second thought to such masculine attention because it wasn't unusual.

Kelsey's beauty had turned male heads ever since her midteens. She had a natural clear-eyed loveliness that dovetailed with her surroundings just then. Like the scenery, her appearance derived from basic assets rather than adornments. Her hair was a natural blond, made even more silvery after weeks in the New Mexico sun. With her tanned skin, it gave her a striking Nordic look, enhanced by the blue of her eyes. High cheekbones emphasized her delicate features, fostering an impression of fragility which was misleading. In twenty-two years, she'd learned to withstand more than one hard knock. The first had come three years ago when her mother and stepfather had been killed in a freeway accident on a holiday weekend. That had left her stepbrother Russ as her only near relative. Russell Dodge was five years older than Kelsey, but they'd an affectionate and harmonious relationship since Kelsey's widowed mother had married Russ's father so many years before. It was

Russ's success in the field of scenery design and model-making which had inspired Kelsey to make it her choice of career as well. And it was Russell she'd come out to visit in Santa Fe some twelve months before when he was working on a classified project at nearby Los Alamos.

Kelsey's expression took on somber lines as she walked back to the house, the morning's mail forgotten in her hand. There hadn't been any warning of impending tragedy on that vacation. She'd been excited at seeing new surroundings and meeting Russ's friends—like Norman Wilkens. Probably the highlight of her visit was being introduced to the chief engineer of Russ's project—a man named Brent Spencer.

Her lips pressed into an unhappy straight line as Brent's face came clearly to mind. It wasn't fair! After a year away from the man, his features should have blurred or vanished—just in common decency. Instead, his stubborn face and his level gray eyes remained as distinct as those in the portrait of a Spanish grandee over her godfather's fireplace.

Brent's glance had taken on even more steely qualities late one night when a phone call alerted him that Russ had just been observed emerging from a restricted section of the Los Alamos complex which housed classified material. Kelsey could still remember Brent's tall figure as he sprinted for his car, calling over his shoulder that he'd be in touch as soon as he had anything definite to report about the break-in.

But it wasn't Brent who told her about Russ's death a few hours later. It was Norman who assumed the unhappy task. And he'd been wonderful. Acting as gently as an older brother himself while he related how Russ's body had been found in his wrecked car on the steep and curving mountain road between Los Alamos and Santa Fe.

"He must have been going fast and lost control," Norman had reported, his freckled countenance mirroring the grief that was in his eyes. At that moment, he hadn't looked like one of Santa Fe's most popular men-about-town; his skin was gray, and his features were bleak and lifeless. But he'd rallied to provide badly needed strength to Kelsey in the weeks that followed. He'd staunchly maintained her stepbrother's innocence even after Brent's official confirmation of the theft and the mounting evidence against Russ in the media. "He wouldn't have taken a book of matches that didn't belong to him," Norman had insisted when newspaper headlines tried and convicted the dead man before government security clamped down.

By then, the strain had taken its toll on Kelsey. Norman went along when she transported her brother's body back to Connecticut for burial, and it was Norman who'd made sure she was on an even keel before leaving her in Manhattan.

Brent hadn't even made an appearance during that hellish time.

Kelsey heard that he'd been called to Washington, D.C., the day after the tragedy, but when the weeks went by without any word, her pride asserted itself. She mailed a stiff little note to his office saying any further communication between them would only resurrect memories that she'd prefer to forget.

There had been two letters from him in the months that followed—official-looking envelopes which she'd returned without opening. By then, she knew that her godfather, who was directing research in Brent's section, would certainly let her know if any new developments occurred. But even he had informed her gruffly that there wasn't much reason to hope for reopening the case. "The boy probably was tempted by some sort of a payoff," he'd told her once over the phone. And then, before she could interrupt, he'd gone on hastily, "It happens, Kelsey. That stepbrother of yours always went through money too fast. Maybe it finally caught up with him."

"I won't believe it. I'll never believe it . . ." she'd said vehemently.

"I know, honey, and I admire your loyalty—but sooner or later, you have to face facts."

Wisely then, he'd changed the subject. When he offered the house-sitting job the following summer probably he felt that returning to Santa Fe might make her face those facts.

It *had* helped her exorcise some of the devils. She was finally able to drive the road to Los Alamos without shuddering, she'd been able to enjoy evenings at the Santa Fe Opera House with Norman as an attentive escort, and even had completed sketches for her next commission in an off-Broadway production.

Her thoughts were still on the sketch she'd done for the show the evening before when an outraged "Wrr-owr" made her jump back from the porch step.

"I'm sorry, Elmo," she said to the cat who'd leaped up on the railing and sat licking his paw. "Let me see it." She drew back as his spine arched,

7

and he uttered a warning rumble. "Well, you needn't get so starchy. I certainly didn't mean to step on you. Maybe some liver would make you feel better."

"Liver" was a word which caught his attention, and he promptly deserted his perch, letting her lead the way into the house.

The sound of a car came vaguely to Kelsey's ears a minute later, but she finished slicing the liver into bite-sized pieces on a saucer in the kitchen, resisting the urge to peer out onto the porch and see who'd stopped by. Probably it was just another motorist who'd gotten thoroughly confused by the dearth of house numbers along Tano Road.

While waiting for the sound of the doorbell, she suddenly became aware of the front door opening and the thud of something heavy being deposited in the entranceway.

Thoroughly alarmed by then, she hurried around the corner to the slate foyer saying, "What are you doing in here . . . ?" Her voice trailed off to an unbecoming gurgle as she recognized the masculine figure stacking another heavy suitcase in the hallway.

Brent Spencer suspended his actions long enough to reach across and steady the saucer of liver as it tilted in her nerveless fingers. "I've already eaten, thanks," he said dryly and then took the saucer as the liver started toward the edge again. "I didn't know raw meat was on your diet these days. Is that another way of proclaiming your independence?"

The color which had drained from Kelsey's face an instant before started seeping back under her cheekbones, and she snatched the saucer from his fingers. "This isn't for me!"

8

His thick dark eyebrows arched. "Company? Maybe I should have phoned first. At this hour of the morning, I didn't think it was necessary." He turned back toward the door, saying over a broad shoulder, "Don't let me interrupt anything."

Kelsey followed him and watched in stunned amazement as he started unloading cardboard cartons from the back of a station wagon parked in the middle of the drive. "What in the devil do you think you're doing?" she finally managed to ask, her voice thin with annoyance.

"Just what it looks like. It's too bad about that," he added, his glance raking her dispassionately. "I did warn you, though."

"Warn me? I don't know what you're talking about."

"The liver. There's a slice of it on your shoe. The rest's down on the tile. Too bad—I'm afraid it's a lost cause. Excuse me—" The last came as he edged past her toward the front door carrying a carton piled high with books.

His exit line was spoiled by a violent hiss when he collided with the tomcat on the threshold. Kelsey watched hopefully as the books shifted and almost fell before Brent salvaged them against his chest.

"What in the hell!" he ground out angrily, trying to see what was happening at ankle level.

"The cat," Kelsey supplied, managing to sound just as dispassionate as he had earlier. She pointed a shapely finger at the threshold, managing to get rid of a remnant of liver decorating her cuticle at the same time. "He likes breakfast about now, so it wasn't a lost cause after all."

The tomcat munched through the bite-sized pieces of liver with deliberate precision while his audience watched.

"I'm sorry I stopped you," Brent told Kelsey finally, letting his gaze come back to hers.

"What do you mean?"

"In the front hall. I presume you were getting ready to toss that liver on the floor when I took the saucer away from you. Lucius didn't tell me he had a cat."

"Well, actually . . ." Kelsey bit her lip, trying for a diplomatic, plausible answer, and then abruptly remembered she didn't need one. "What difference does it make to you? I don't know what you think you're doing here, but you can just move that stuff right back in the station wagon and head down the road. Lucius asked me to take care of his house a long time ago . . ."

"He asked me last week."

". . . so it doesn't matter how many cats I want to feed or where I want to feed them—" Her voice faltered. "What did you say?" she asked after the silence had lengthened and he made no attempt to break it.

"I said that he got in touch with me last week. He didn't want the house empty, and he can't get back from Brussels until the middle of September." Brent reached into the pocket of his cotton slacks and hefted the door key on his palm. "How do you suppose I got this? I wasn't sure whether you'd still be here or on your way to Mexico."

From his complete lack of expression, Kelsey could tell that her presence wasn't going to affect his plans

10

one way or the other. She felt a tremor of fear mingle with the anger that already had her clenching her fists at her side. All along she'd known that she'd have to meet Brent again—it was a foregone conclusion in such a small place as Santa Fe. But she'd learned on her arrival that he was traveling abroad, and since she'd not wanted to show any special interest, she'd let the matter rest.

Not that it made any real difference, she told herself. It just would have been easier if she'd been prepared. She could have been dressed decently, for one thing, instead of appearing in old khaki pants that were too tight and a blue chambray work shirt she donned to wash the car.

Naturally, Brent was as immaculate as she'd remembered. Faded blue denims fitted without a wrinkle at his slim hips and a dark blue sport shirt was open at the throat revealing the tan that he had probably acquired from sitting beside a European swimming pool. His thick dark hair was as much under control as every other part of the man, she thought resentfully. Only the wrinkles at the corners of his eyes and the frown line that seemed a permanent feature between his eyebrows showed that the months they'd been apart had left their mark. She drew a guilty breath as she encountered his brooding look, uncomfortably aware that he had been surveying her appearance with a far more uncharitable conclusion.

That thought shattered most of the remnants of her poise. The final bits disintegrated when he hefted a suitcase and said, "Which way to the bedroom?"

"Down here . . ." She automatically gestured to

the hall and then her hand went up to her lips, stricken by this new development. "But you can't stay here."

"Why not?" he asked, pulling up halfway down the hall. "Isn't your stuff out yet?"

"No, it isn't."

Before she could say anymore, he shrugged and added, "Well, I'll stack my belongings in the corner until you're on your way. How long will it take you?"

Kelsey started to say that she had no intention of leaving—no matter what he thought—when there was another complaining "Mrr-owr" from the front door. The cat stalked toward them, still licking his whiskers.

"Your friend isn't happy," Brent observed. "He must still be hungry."

"Just annoyed. His appetizer escaped this morning," Kelsey replied, her attention still on more important problems. "He's a 'bring 'em back alive' type."

"I suggest you wean him to kibbled biscuit. Preferably served *in* a saucer—not *on* the floor. I'll even donate the dish when you both leave."

"That's just it," she cut in desperately before things got even further out of hand. "He's not leaving. I mean, I don't know what he's going to do." She bent over stroking the rough head as the tomcat wound around her ankles.

"Try to get more breakfast. Anyone could see that."

Anger made her stiffen indignantly. "Will you listen! I'm trying to tell you that *I'm* not going any-

12

place either. This whole thing is a misunderstanding on your part."

Brent frowned at her and then started down the hall again, saying over his shoulder, "If there's any misunderstanding—it's in your head. Lucius and I know exactly what's going on. We settled it in Brussels the other day. I'm moving in until he's finished over there. You weren't mentioned—except in passing," he added negligently, pausing at the open bedroom door and surveying the room with an approving expression.

Kelsey stepped over the cat and hurried after him down the hall as he disappeared in the bedroom. "Wait a minute! You have to listen to me."

He turned back, looking as if he'd much rather continue surveying the attractive master bedroom with its camel-colored carpet and slate-blue spread on the big double bed. Two comfortable armchairs were upholstered in a print with the same shade of blue predominating and the material was repeated in draperies at the floor-to-ceiling window which overlooked the valley and mountains beyond. "I'm listening," he said as he stood by the window. "Make it quick, though. I'm expecting Geraldine any minute."

"Your secretary? Why? What's she coming for?" The prospect of Geraldine Laser's arrival was a new low in the morning's developments. Even so, Brent's expression showed Kelsey that she'd better backtrack if she expected any answers. "I merely meant that I was surprised," she stammered, "since you've just arrived and all. Unless she was with you in Europe."

Brent moved then, taking his suitcase and deposit-

13

ing it by the closet door. "She wasn't. She just met me at the airport in Albuquerque this morning. I wasn't sure that the station wagon was entirely trustworthy so she followed me to Santa Fe in her car. Any more questions?" The last came as he walked back to her and leaned against the door. "No? Then maybe you can answer one for me. What in the devil's going on in that mind of yours now? Is this some sort of 'sit-in' you're planning just to make things more difficult?"

"Of course not. Lucius doesn't know that my Mexican trip was called off."

"Why not?"

"Because I didn't have time to tell him, that's all. There wasn't any great crashing rush. He didn't tell me about your coming. Or Geraldine's."

The last two words were delivered so bitterly that Kelsey might as well have written a placard saying "I can't stand the woman" and pasted it on the wall. In all the months she'd been away from Santa Fe, she hadn't forgotten the secretary's testimony at the time of the office break-in. Geraldine Laser had been at the forefront in naming Russ as the guilty party.

"Lucius didn't have anything to do with Geraldine's arrival," Brent commented dryly. "I just phoned her between planes about meeting me. And to set the record straight—she isn't my secretary any longer. She hasn't been for some months."

"I'm surprised." Kelsey kept her voice level with an effort. "Don't tell me you parted company voluntarily?"

"That cat of yours isn't the only one who's sharpening his claws," Brent observed. "For what it's

14

worth—I switched to a solar-energy project, and Geraldine's working for the man who took over my old job."

"Lucius didn't mention it."

"Probably he didn't think you'd be interested. Your friend Norman emphasized several times that you didn't want anything to do with your old—acquaintances."

Kelsey flushed uncomfortably as he drawled out the last word. It occurred to her that she could have acted too impulsively those months before—it might have been wiser to deal with the aftermath herself rather than hiding behind her grief. That realization made her tone defensive as she said, "Well, at least Lucius could have told me that you were arriving today."

"Oh, for Lord's sake—be reasonable, Kelsey. He thought you'd left. That's why he furnished a duplicate house key. Incidentally, don't forget to give me yours when you leave this morning."

"This morning?" Kelsey laughed scornfully. "You obviously haven't consulted a calendar—it's the middle of the Arts Festival here. The place is bulging at the seams and has been for weeks. There's opera and chamber music scheduled, plus the Indian Market, and a fiesta starting soon."

Brent appeared slightly stunned by her recital but only for a moment. "I can see where it presents a problem. What about some of your friends?"

She chewed unhappily on her lower lip. "I don't know many people here. At least not well enough to ask to live with them."

"What about your pal Wilkens? Or has he been bunking up here since you've been in town?"

Her voice was tight as she flared back, "Don't judge me by your standards—or dear Geraldine's. My God! She's a fund of misinformation, isn't she?"

"Geraldine doesn't even come into this. Just because she happened to be my secretary doesn't mean that she"—he hesitated to find the right word—"helps out in other ways. Your name wasn't mentioned when she met me at the airport."

Kelsey's response was an unladylike snort. "That's a switch, at least. She had plenty to say the last time I was here."

"Not about you. And she shouldn't be blamed for her testimony about the break-in. She was just reporting facts."

"And I say she lied in her teeth. Russ wasn't a thief! You'll never make me believe it." Kelsey drew in a trembling breath. "I don't care what evidence they found in his car."

Brent looked uncomfortable to be digging up the old bone of contention. "If you'd ever let me discuss it with you—we wouldn't still be fighting after all this time."

"You weren't around that week," she said, her tone stiff and unyielding. "Or have you forgotten?"

"I haven't forgotten," he bit back, his eyes narrowing angrily. "You had plenty of help—I remember that, too."

"Norman was wonderful," she said, matching his tone. "And he believed in Russ. He still does."

"Great. Maybe he's equally talented in finding vacant real estate." Brent headed down the hall again to pick up another armful of his belongings.

"You'll have to give me more time," Kelsey protested, trailing him. "If you have one decent bone in your body—you'll find a place to stay for a day or two. At least until I get things under control."

"No way." Brent tossed his raincoat over his shoulder and grabbed a bulging attaché case before starting toward the bedroom again. He carefully avoided the big tomcat who was watching their parade route, and Kelsey also detoured around the feline reviewing stand as she followed.

"You needn't be so stubborn," she said, trying to catch up. "It wouldn't hurt you just this once . . ."

Brent put his attaché case at the end of the bed and slid open the closet door, looking for a spare hanger. Not finding any, he pulled her seersucker robe from one, draping it over a blouse on an adjoining hanger, and settled his raincoat in the vacant space.

"Make yourself right at home," Kelsey said through gritted teeth as she watched the maneuver. "Do you intend to toss my entire wardrobe out the door or does that come later?"

"You always did have a tendency to dramatize things." Brent lifted his smaller suitcase onto the bed and opened it. He took out a shaving kit before starting toward the adjoining bathroom.

Kelsey followed him grimly, thinking that she'd had more than her share of his broad back in the last few minutes. "Wait a minute—you can't root around in the medicine cabinet. That's my toothbrush! And my soap!"

"Exactly." Brent swept them onto the marble

17

counter. "But *my* medicine cabinet." He shoved aside a bottle of bath crystals to put his gear on the shelf.

"*Will* you listen to me!" In her annoyance, Kelsey stamped her foot and then felt like a fool as Brent bestowed a pitying look.

"I *have* been listening to you," he pointed out. "Ever since I arrived."

"Well, then—stop cleaning house for a minute . . ."

He stepped back and folded his arms over his chest. "That's the least of my concerns right now. Unless you've been dumping chopped liver around in here, as well."

"Only when the moon is full and I'm expecting company," she said with a clenched jaw. "You're safe for the moment. Is there any reason I can't occupy the guest bedroom until I can find another place to live?"

He stared at her. "Talk about a loaded question—that's like asking me if I beat women regularly. What do you really want to know?"

"If you've already invited company."

"Geraldine won't be sleeping in," he announced. "So you don't have to worry on that score at the moment."

"Well, then . . ."

He cut her off before she could finish. "But I have some house rules that you'd better know. The guest room is strictly for solo occupancy. Or don't I have to worry about that?"

"Not at the moment," she said, quoting him deliberately and hoping she sounded just as nasty. He was well aware that she had never shared the premises and

18

didn't intend to. The Brent she'd known all those months before wouldn't have thought of such sarcastic innuendos, let alone mention them. "You needn't worry, I'll get out of here as soon as possible."

He rubbed his jaw with his thumb, staring at her in such a way that Kelsey wished for the umpteenth time that she'd managed to run a comb through her hair and put on some lipstick before their confrontation. To break the silence, she added her toothbrush to the slippery stack of her belongings and said, "I'll transfer these to the other bath."

He nodded almost absently, gathering a few more of her things on the shelves and following her down the hallway the few feet to the adjoining guest bathroom. As he watched her put the bath crystals away, he finally said, "I've been thinking. Maybe you won't have to search for another place to live, after all."

Kelsey was so surprised that she had to swallow over the sudden dryness in her throat. "I don't understand. Why the change of heart?"

He didn't hesitate to set her straight. "My heart hasn't anything to do with it. I'm just looking at it from a practical standpoint. Probably she could use some company on the scene."

"I thought you said that Geraldine wasn't involved?" Kelsey slammed her toothbrush onto the shelf so hard that it vibrated. "I'm not going to stay here with her even if it means sleeping on the grass in the town square."

"Nobody's asking you to." He slid a plastic glass across the counter hastily, as if getting it out of reach. "Geraldine's just bringing Daisy from the airport."

"Daisy! My God, who's Daisy?" Kelsey asked, feeling as if she'd just been hit hard in the stomach. Then she said accusingly, "Elmo, you're not supposed to do that." The last was directed to the tomcat who'd decided to join the action and leaped up on the edge of the wash basin.

Brent added a forceful "Get down from there!" but when the cat didn't move, he turned to Kelsey. "What the hell did you say his name was?"

"Elmo." She put a gentle but determined hand at the base of the tomcat's tail and pushed. "Down, boy." Then she turned back to Brent who was shaking his head unbelievingly. "What's the matter?"

"Elmo! My Lord, what a name for—" He gestured toward the disappearing cat. "For that!"

"He doesn't complain." Kelsey's tone was cold. "How about your friend Daisy? Is she used to cats?"

Brent started to answer and then closed his mouth again, obviously thinking it over. "Do you know—I didn't have a chance to ask her," he said finally. "Offhand, I wouldn't imagine she'd be too keen. Maybe you can keep Elmo away from her."

"I'll do my best." Privately Kelsey decided that her best would be none too good. If Brent was idiot enough to be entertaining a woman who didn't like animals, then he might as well see her true side. "You can't expect me not to feed him."

"Elmo is missing lots of things but food isn't one of them. You must have thrown half a pound of liver on the floor." Brent started down the hall toward the

20

foyer again, "You'd better order some more for dinner. *My* dinner. I know Daisy likes it, too."

To her annoyance, Kelsey found herself at his heels again. "*Would* you stop trotting up and down this hall like a marathon runner. There's a perfectly good living room in here with chairs where we can discuss this like two sensible adults."

"I didn't think there was anything more to talk about."

"That's where you're wrong," Kelsey informed him coldly. She gestured in to the attractive living room where a floor-to-ceiling window covered most of the far wall, overlooking acres of piñon pine and juniper in the gently rolling countryside. There were a few contemporary homes nestled in the landscape, but the general impression was of space and sunshine topped with a clear cobalt sky. The room's monochromatic tone of beige for the carpet and furniture added to the untrammeled atmosphere. There was only the rust coloring of the fireplace brick, picked up again in accent pillows to provide a dash of warmth, and it blended easily with the copper-tiled kitchen visible around the corner.

Brent gave a low whistle of approval as he surveyed the pleasant surroundings. "Lucius does well for himself. Or did he inherit the color scheme from the former owners?"

"Some of it. He asked me to do a little fixing while I was here."

"You haven't lost your knack. Maybe you should have concentrated on decorating instead of set design."

"Russ thought the other would be more fulfilling

as a career. I haven't been sorry that I switched over."

"Your stepbrother was a good judge of talent." Brent's expression was hooded. "I'm sure that your career is a rousing success by now. Lucius mentioned it a few days ago."

There was something in his voice that caused Kelsey to make a deprecating gesture. "There are lots of talented people humming around Broadway. And a lot of them here in Santa Fe during the festival who could give me a run for my money. Actually, I enjoyed decorating this house for Lucius—it gave me a chance to pay him back for his hospitality."

"Well, if you're still feeling generous, I could use some help entertaining Daisy. New Mexico is a far cry from the midlands of England."

Jealousy closed over Kelsey like a suffocating cloak but she tried to be tactful. "I can't promise anything long term. In two or three days, I should dig up another place to stay. Norman probably will know of something."

Brent's jaw hardened. "I wondered how long it would be before he came into the picture. Or if he'd ever left it."

His sarcasm made Kelsey blink. "What's that supposed to mean?"

"Think about it for a while. In the meantime, do me a favor and keep him as far away from here as possible."

"Let me get this straight! I'm supposed to stay here and entertain your latest heartthrob, but I can't even be decent to a man who's been a wonderful friend."

"Spare the adjectives. I've heard them before." Brent got to his feet with his characteristic economy of movement. "Frankly I don't give a damn how you treat him—just so you don't do it in front of me."

Kelsey drew herself up stiffly, making no attempt to hide her anger. "This will never work. I'm not staying here. You can do what you want with your precious Daisy—" She broke off as he gestured abruptly. "What now?"

"I heard a car. It must be Geraldine."

"Big deal."

Kelsey's irritable mutter was just loud enough for Brent to hear. He leveled a look that was meant to shrivel as he started down the hallway. "You'd better come along."

Only a determination not to be found hiding inside like some Victorian parlor maid made her follow his suggestion. She walked slowly toward the door, deciding that she would greet the woman in a polite offhand manner that no one could fault. She shook her head at the irony of it—it was a textbook case of "off with the old and on with the new" whether Brent realized it or not. She could only hope his precious Daisy didn't, either.

Geraldine must have, though. At least something was responsible for her tight-lipped, annoyed expression as she stormed into the hallway and ran a calculating glance over Kelsey. "Brent just told me you were here. Did you come to blow on the coals or rake over the ashes?"

The humor of the situation finally struck Kelsey.

"Does it matter? Daisy is the only one on Brent's mind right now."

"Well, you obviously didn't dress for the occasion." Geraldine unconsciously smoothed the collar of her teal-blue blouse which was a perfect match for her well-fitting pants suit. Kelsey recalled that the secretary had always chosen clothes carefully to accentuate her trim figure. She still wore her dark hair at shoulder length but just then it was drawn back from her face and she'd pushed her sunglasses atop her head in casual fashion. There was nothing casual about her light-blue-eyed glance, though, and her mouth was petulant.

"Believe it or not, I didn't have any idea we were holding an open house," Kelsey said, keeping her voice light. "Would you like some coffee while you're here? I'm going in and pack."

"You mean you aren't staying? Brent didn't say anything about that."

"He just found out. Probably he's so taken up with Daisy's arrival that he forgot to mention it."

"Well, he's welcome to her," Geraldine said, entering the kitchen to get herself a mug and pour coffee from the percolator on the stove. "She didn't pay any attention to me from the minute I picked her up at the airport. I think Brent's out of his mind."

Kelsey lingered in the archway. Hearing Geraldine go on about Brent's newest love was like probing for a suspected cavity—it hurt like the dickens but there was no disguising the necessity. "She's English, isn't she?"

Geraldine nodded. "Very blue-blood. That's part

of her appeal, I suppose. Brent's hoping for great things."

"He *has* changed. That wouldn't have influenced him before."

"You'll find he has a lot of new ideas," Geraldine reverted to her usual smug tones. "What did you expect after you did your disappearing act? No man worth having is going to sit around waiting for a woman to come back to him. Especially not a man like Brent." She inspected her cuticle carefully and frowned. "If you ask me, I think you left it a little late."

"But then nobody's asking you, Gerry." It was Brent who made that calm pronouncement as he appeared in the kitchen archway. He didn't let the silence lengthen, turning instead to frown at Kelsey. "I thought you were coming out to see Daisy."

"Well—" Kelsey pushed a strand of hair back with a nervous gesture. "I can, of course. But why don't you bring her in?"

"She wanted a little exercise. Incidentally, you'll have to do something about that damned cat. He took a swipe at my ankle while I was helping her out of the car. I don't want him bothering Daisy—she's unstrung enough after such a long flight."

It wasn't an unreasonable request and Kelsey could only nod unhappily. She'd have to persuade one of the neighbors up the road to feed Elmo when she left. "I'll do what I can." She rubbed her hands down the sides of her rumpled pants. "I'm sorry that I'm not more presentable."

"That's all right. Daisy's sort of a mess, too." Geraldine was still cradling her coffee mug as she leaned against the refrigerator.

Brent shot her another annoyed glance before he opened the front door and waved Kelsey ahead of him onto the porch. "Deliver me from the female of the species," he muttered under his breath.

Kelsey's spirits surged at that comment but her expression became puzzled at the sight of the empty drive. "I don't see anybody. She didn't decide to go for a walk on Tano Road, did she?"

"I sure as hell hope not." Brent strode toward Geraldine's hatchback, parked behind his station wagon.

Bewildered, Kelsey turned to Geraldine who was lounging in the front doorway, still nursing her coffee. "I should think she'd want to come in and wash off the travel stains."

"My thought exactly and she has plenty of territory to wash." The secretary's thin lips quirked in amusement as her glance shifted to the drive. "Well, the lost is found. That should make Brent happier. Even Daisy looks more cheerful."

Kelsey took a deep breath to steady herself and tried to put a welcoming expression on her face as she turned around to greet the newcomer. But instead of the trim female she expected, there was a large and dusty dog stalking unhappily at Brent's side. "Good Lord!" Kelsey murmured, "That's Daisy?"

"That's Daisy," Geraldine confirmed.

Brent tightened the leash and brought the dog alongside him with some difficulty, pulling up beside the porch. He noted Kelsey's expression with

26

annoyance. "If you'd been traveling as long as she has—you wouldn't look too great either."

Kelsey waved that aside as she walked over to the shaggy animal who looked more like a disreputable teddy bear than anything else. She extended her fist slowly toward the black rubber stamp of a nose.

Daisy took one look through her drooping eyebrows and promptly put her head down, out of range.

Kelsey frowned as she surveyed the brownish dog more carefully. Then she turned her head and said wonderingly to Brent. "There's an Airedale underneath all that hair and dirt, isn't there? Where on earth did you find her?"

"A kennel in England." Brent was watching the two of them but his expression was impassive. "She's five years old. They were about to put her to sleep because she couldn't be bred. I found her in a run at the back of the place."

"The poor soul!" Kelsey looked down at the disconsolate creature who was staring at the ground. "Well, something has to be done with her—that's for sure."

"I couldn't desert her after I heard the story but dammit—I don't know anything about taking care of dogs. Maybe you can find a decent boarding kennel for her before you leave."

Geraldine broke in eagerly, "If that's all you want, I can ask around."

"Don't bother." Kelsey reached for the Airedale's leash with sudden determination. "Daisy isn't going to any boarding kennel."

Brent was watching her intently. "You know what

that means? You have to stick around to look out for her."

There was a sound of pottery breaking as Geraldine's coffee mug hit the porch tiles. "Sorry. It slipped," she said, making no attempt to pick up the pieces. "Now that everything's settled, you won't need me any longer."

Kelsey was trying to quiet the big dog who had shied nervously at the sound of breaking crockery. She took an instant, though, to look up and say tersely to the other woman, "That's right, Geraldine. We won't need you any longer."

Chapter 2

⟨⟩

It was perhaps five minutes before Brent came back back into the house after seeing Geraldine off in her car. He ran Kelsey to earth in the utility room where she had tethered the exhausted Daisy to the leg of a laundry tub while she searched through some towels stacked nearby.

"You were a little hard on her, weren't you?" Brent asked, walking over to pet the dog who stood like a small horse.

Kelsey gave him a brief glance before going back to her sorting task. "I don't want to let her loose now before I give her a bath. If I had to chase her around the house, it wouldn't help her state of mind."

"I'm not talking about Daisy," he said.

"Oh." Kelsey looked blank for a moment as if she had no idea what he was talking about. Then her brow cleared. "You mean Geraldine? All I did was tell the truth. She wouldn't be any help at all. Do you suppose Lucius would care if Daisy used some of his good towels?"

Brent surveyed the two thick coral bath towels she

was holding and shrugged. "Go ahead. We can replace them. Daisy's due for a treat."

"She won't think a shower's much of a thrill." Kelsey picked up a bottle of shampoo and went across the room to survey the utility shower stall. "You're going to have to hold her."

He looked blank. "My God, you mean get in with her?"

"Well, one of us has to. The other one can do the soaping. Either way, we get wet—so you'd better put on some other clothes."

Brent shook his head. "No need. Everything I have on is washable and I have to change later anyhow. Before I take Geraldine out to dinner," he explained, seeing Kelsey's puzzled look.

"Tonight?"

"That's right." He tightened his grip on Daisy when the dog suddenly started struggling. "She must be allergic to baths."

"Geraldine?" Kelsey inquired silkily and then blushed under Brent's reproving glance. "You keep changing the subject so fast it's hard to keep up. As far as Daisy goes, I doubt if she can remember that far back."

"Well, it looks as if we're going to have a devil of a time holding her in that shower stall. Of course, you're the expert at this," he went on conversationally. "Didn't you tell me that you handled show dogs on the circuit during your vacations from college?"

"I did more grooming than handling." Kelsey was preocccupied but had time to wonder how Brent recalled such vague snippets of information. Not that she had forgotten the things he'd confided in their early acquaintance, either. It was only during the recent months that she'd wished she could.

"Daisy's not going to wait around while you go into a fog. She's about to choke herself now."

"I know. She's scared to death. It's a shame she has to be bathed but right now she's pretty grim. Come on, girl—nobody will hurt you. Just stand there a minute longer," Kelsey went on in a calm voice, "and I'll bring you a surprise."

"Hold on—there's time to make friends with her later," Brent protested as Kelsey turned for the hallway. "Are you going to put her in this shower or not?"

"I'll be back in a minute. Instead of losing your temper, just pet the poor thing and talk to her. Nicely," Kelsey admonished before she disappeared around the door.

A moment later, she was back, holding a squirming Elmo in her arms.

"Damn it, Kelsey, this isn't a communal bath-house!" Brent exploded.

She paid no attention, carefully putting the cat down close to the unhappy dog. "Look here, Daisy. How would you like a roommate?"

"You think he's a selling point?" Brent jibed.

"Well—right now she's so busy watching him that she's forgotten to fight the leash," Kelsey said as she took the braided leather from him. Slipping off her flat sandals she led the dog into the shower enclosure. "Hold still, girl. Brent, test the temperature of the water, will you?"

"Right." He was watching the proceedings with a bemused expression. "It's a good thing you have this

31

telephone shower gimmick or you'd be wetter than Daisy by now."

Kelsey nodded and took the chrome fitting from him, directing the tepid stream onto the cringing dog. "There you are, Daisy. That doesn't hurt, does it? In a minute or so, you'll be clean and beautiful."

"At least clean," Brent said ruefully, offering the shampoo bottle.

"More than that." Avoiding Daisy's eyes, Kelsey worked the shampoo into a lather on the thick coat. "I think that under this hippie hairdo, there's a darned good-looking dog."

"Maybe that's why Elmo's still sticking around." Brent nodded toward the counter where the tomcat sat watching them.

"Either that or it's because he had an invitation. Most of the time, he's booted out in this neighborhood."

"Another survivor, huh?" Brent's sympathetic grin made him look younger and more approachable suddenly. "You hear that, Daisy? There's a kindred soul over there."

Since the object of his remarks was being thoroughly rinsed just then, she didn't look ecstatic at the information. She did remain quiet, however—even staying in place when the water was finally turned off and the coral towels were brought into use.

"Close that door over there so she can't get out, please," Kelsey told Brent. "I'll let her off the leash now and turn on the ceiling heater. She and Elmo can practice co-existence until she's thoroughly dry—" She broke off as Daisy celebrated her freedom by dashing into the middle of the room and shaking vigorously.

The spray made Brent wince and sent Elmo up to a shelf out of range. Surprised to find herself at liberty, Daisy looked around hesitantly and then walked over to peer up at the cat.

"My Lord, she wagged her tail."

The profound awe in Brent's words made Kelsey giggle. "You make it sound like a papal pronouncement."

"Hardly in the same category. All the same, it's nice to know that her tail goes up as well as down. I didn't think she even knew how to move it." Brent took another look at the scruffy cat. "I can't say much for her taste."

"He has hidden assets." Kelsey set the thermostat on the overhead heater while Daisy sat down on an old folded bedspread and started licking her paws. "I think everything's under control for the moment. Later on, you'll have to get her fitted out."

"What do you mean?"

"All the necessities. A bed, dog food, and dishes—" Kelsey hesitated as he tried to hide his amusement, and then went on coolly, "I don't use the floor for feeding dogs. Elmo's unique."

"That he is," Brent agreed, his gaze on the cat who was settling onto a coiled extension cord. "How did he get the name Elmo?"

"What's wrong with Elmo?" Kelsey asked, trying to keep a straight face.

"I should have known better than to ask. At least he's captured Daisy's interest for the moment," Brent said in an undertone, following Kelsey out into the hallway and closing the door firmly behind them. "Is there any more of that coffee around?"

"There should be unless Geraldine smashed the pot."

"She wasn't *that* unhappy when she left."

"I imagine a date for dinner soothed her feelings. She always impressed me as the practical type," Kelsey said, trying to keep the bitterness from her voice but not succeeding too well.

The cheerful surroundings of the kitchen made it easier to overlook the unpleasant happenings of the morning. Sunshine streamed through the big windows onto the bank of hickory cabinets and the copper tile of the countertop. Kelsey opened a cupboard door and found a mug so that Brent could help himself to the coffee.

After he'd poured it, he glanced around the sunlit room and nodded approvingly. "Very nice. Is this another of your projects?"

He was being so agreeable that Kelsey regretted the uncharitable thoughts that were occupying her mind. Of course, he could afford to be magnanimous; he had a beautiful brunette eager to have dinner with him and in the meantime he'd neatly arranged a live-in housekeeper and dog-sitter. Only a muffled "woof" from the utility room showed that Daisy wouldn't be happy in her confinement much longer.

"Hadn't we better be doing something?" Brent asked, apparently aware of that protesting "woof," as well.

Kelsey nodded and started toward the bedroom. "I'm going in and change clothes. Daisy will have

34

to tough it out for a few minutes longer. I can move into the guest room after I come back from town."

"Hold on a minute." Brent didn't waste any time pursuing her down the hallway. "You mean you're going into Santa Fe this morning?"

The sound of the front doorbell cut into his last word.

Kelsey lingered on the threshold of the bedroom, not looking forward to his reaction to her next declaration. "*We're* going into Santa Fe. That is, if you'll answer the door and tell Norman I'll be ready in five minutes."

Brent's eyebrows met in a forbidding line. "Wilkens is here?"

The doorbell sounded again, plus an impatient rapping on the door that set off frantic barking from the utility room, together with the sound of a paw splintering wood.

"I'm sorry," Kelsey said, taking the coward's way out, "but I really have to get out of these clothes."

Brent did the only thing he could do under the circumstances. He waved her impatiently into the bedroom. "Go ahead. I'll let him in and give him some coffee." He winced as the paw could be heard again. "I'd better get Daisy out before she tears that door to shreds."

Kelsey managed to nod and close the bedroom door behind her, waiting until it was safely shut before her lips curved upward in a pleased smile. It was almost worth the heartbreak to see Brent's customary assurance ravel at the edges. She'd known that he disliked Norman but his outright hostility came as a surprise.

He was simply overreacting, Kelsey told herself, as she hurried to the closet and pulled a skirt and blouse from the hanger. Detouring by the bureau, she rummaged for clean underthings and went on into the bath.

A thud suddenly reverberated through the house and then Brent could be heard shouting, "Daisy! Cut that out and get down!" There was a silence, followed immediately by the sound of paws skittering past in the slate hallway.

Kelsey grimaced and reached for the shower faucet, but not before she heard Norman's voice raised querulously. "Why in the hell didn't you warn me? How am I supposed to get muddy pawprints off gabardine?"

Kelsey turned on the water full force. With any luck, Brent would have the mud off Daisy's paws by the time she reappeared. Although how the dog managed to find dirt in the utility room was a mystery.

Brent offered a simple solution fifteen minutes later when Kelsey appeared in the living room wearing clean clothes and with her hair gleaming. "Where's Norman?" she asked, seeing only Daisy beside him.

"Out on the porch with a whisk broom trying to accomplish the impossible. I told him you would understand about the mud on his trousers but it didn't help his temper."

Kelsey surveyed the big dog who was staring morosely into the fireplace, clearly tempted by the ashes. "Don't get any ideas," Kelsey told her firmly. "How did you manage to make mud pies in the utility room?"

"She had help from the cat. He knocked down that bag of potting soil and then started playing tag with the dog."

Kelsey closed her eyes, visualizing the chaos and wondering how long it would take to clean up. "You didn't plan bringing a small horse to board, too? As long as we're in the business."

"There are advantages to a horse." The comment came from the man who appeared suddenly in the hall. He came on in and dropped a whisk broom on an end table gesturing angrily at his trousers which still bore remnants of grime. "You could have warned me."

"Norman, I'm sorry." Kelsey felt like holding her head as she saw the anger on his usually placid countenance. "Honestly, I didn't have time." A heavy silence followed her apology and it didn't take a clairvoyant to determine that neither man was going to break it. "You remember Brent, of course."

"Naturally. But I didn't know you were expecting company."

"Not exactly company," Brent corrected. "I'm occupying the house for Lucius until he comes back to Santa Fe. Kelsey forgot to tell him that she was staying on."

To say that Norman looked disconcerted was putting it mildly. Although in his early thirties, his fair coloring and slight but wiry frame made him look much younger. At that moment, however, his angry reaction to Brent's words reversed the trend. During the past year, his lighthearted approach to life had made Kelsey feel an easy comaraderie with him. It was a surprise to learn that a few pawprints

37

would put him in such a tizzy. "You should have seen me before I changed," she told him gently. "I think I got more of a shower bath than poor Daisy."

"You mean you were actually *in* with that dog?" Norman's voice, which had a tendency to go high in pitch when he was excited followed its usual course.

"Well, we weren't rolling around together," Kelsey retorted in some annoyance. She was doing her best to exhibit sympathy for his plight but he wasn't making it easy by such a stiff-necked attitude and the tension in the room wasn't improved by Brent's poorly concealed amusement. "Daisy won't be as difficult when she's gotten used to her surroundings," she added.

Norman shrugged. "I don't see what that has to do with you. Or did you forget that we had a date for lunch before the rehearsal?"

"I hadn't forgotten—I just didn't have time to remember."

"I'm afraid there are some complications," Brent said. "I have to drive up to Los Alamos and report in. That's why I recruited Kelsey's services earlier."

Norman stiffened with anger. Since Brent towered over him by a good six inches, the gesture wasn't as effective as it might have been. Kelsey found herself wishing that he'd drop his bantam-cock stance and act more like his usual self. Instead he proclaimed belligerently, "Kelsey doesn't have any spare time. If she did, there are plenty of jobs available here in her field."

"Norman—I wish you'd let me get a word in edgewise," Kelsey protested, feeling the tension in the air.

Even the big dog at Brent's side seemed aware of it. She eyed Norman across the room and then looked up at the man holding her leash as if for reassurance.

"This isn't getting us anywhere," Kelsey started again, only to have Brent interrupt brusquely.

"You'll have to continue this without me," he said towing the reluctant dog with him as he came across to Kelsey and handed her the leash. "I'll be back later this afternoon but not for long. Keep track of how much you spend on Daisy and I'll reimburse you. Sorry I can't stick around, Norman," he added as an obvious afterthought from the hallway. "Ask Kelsey to give you another cup of coffee before you leave."

"Well, I like that!" Norman said wrathfully a second after the front door slammed. "Who in the hell does he think he is?"

"The man who runs this house—for the moment."

Color surged in Norman's thin face. "He may have bought the dog but I didn't think you were for sale. Correct me if I'm wrong."

"As a rule, I don't fight with a man when he's going to pay for my lunch," Kelsey said, corralling her annoyance with an effort. In the background, she could hear Brent starting his car and then driving off.

"You haven't answered my question," Norman insisted.

"On the other hand, there's a great deal to be said for eating a peanut butter sandwich with just Daisy for company."

"Don't be ridiculous! Go put her in the garage or someplace and let's get going!" Norman shoved his hands in his pockets and made an effort to reclaim his poise. "I'm sorry, Kelsey. There's something about that guy that makes me . . ."

". . . lose your temper. I take it that I'm to eat peanut butter another day." Kelsey perched on the end of the beige sofa.

"Of course. Will you be coming back here afterwards?" he asked, starting to move over beside her and then prudently staying away from the dog's wet black nose.

"I don't have anywhere else to go for the moment. That's why Brent was giving orders. For the next week or so, I'm the resident housekeeper and dog-sitter."

"And in return?"

"I just get a roof over my head and a chance to raid the refrigerator." Her voice was level—dangerously so. "If you keep on this way, I'm tempted to let go of Daisy's leash. She's the only one on my side right now."

"Well, you can hardly expect me to be enchanted with this situation." When she didn't answer he said weakly, "I thought we were—friends."

"Friends trust each other. And also accept an uninvited guest for lunch."

"My God, you don't mean it! Take that bale of hair into town! I'd be the laughingstock of everybody I meet."

"All she needs is to be trimmed."

"And to lose about twenty pounds."

"Half of Santa Fe fits into that category. Look, I can't leave her here alone. She'd probably chase Elmo all over the house." Kelsey gestured toward the cat

40

who was stalking toward the front door. "Even if Elmo wanted to stay—which he doesn't."

"Elmo?" Norman sounded dazed.

"The cat. Let him out, will you—while I get my purse." She kept a firm hand on the leash as she tugged the dog toward the bedroom.

"Why didn't you warn me?" Norman asked irritably when she emerged a moment later. He was rubbing his ankle by the open front door and straightened with some effort.

She stared blankly. "Against what?"

"That lousy cat! He clawed me when I shoved him out the door."

"I'm sorry . . ."

"Oh, hell, forget it. You're sure you're ready now? Both of you?" He directed a baleful glance at Daisy who didn't appear enchanted by the coming journey either.

"Maybe we should take my car," Kelsey said, thinking aloud. "I'm not sure how the dog rides." When Norman looked perplexed, she added, "Daisy might get car-sick or leap around."

"I'll take my chances. After everything that's happened so far, I'm getting numb." He motioned her and the dog ahead of him through the door. "I'm drawing the line if she wants to drive, though."

"I should hope so," Kelsey agreed, happy that the atmosphere had lightened. "After all, there's no use taking chances."

"My feeling exactly."

"Especially as Daisy doesn't have her New Mexico license yet." When Norman's eyes widened, she shrugged apologetically. "Sorry, it's been a rough morning."

The rest of the forenoon wasn't appreciably better. Fortunately, Daisy lay quietly, sunk in apathy at being in another moving vehicle. Since she wasn't any trouble, Kelsey was able to soothe Norman's ego, inquiring about his television commercials for a local savings and loan. "Is there any hope of a series from it?"

"Not with their current budget," he groused. "It's just a good thing that I have some other income."

"That's an understatement—considering the amount of real estate you own in town."

"Right now, I wish I had an empty apartment," he replied, refusing to be mollified. "Then you could tell Brent exactly where to go. Don't worry, though. I'll ask around this afternoon at the rehearsal. Maybe somebody will know of a vacant place."

"I'll be all right. You have enough on your mind with that benefit coming up," she assured him. Since he was a leading light in local theater, he was directing a benefit performance at the famed Santa Fe Opera House featuring student-apprentice singers. Norman was enjoying the task enormously and Kelsey had been glad to assist when he'd asked her advice on stage settings and program notes.

"I suppose you won't be able to attend the rehearsal this afternoon," he said, turning off the freeway onto a two-lane road which led past some new condominiums on the way to town. "Unless you could park that dog"—he jerked his head toward the rear seat—"in a kennel someplace.'"

Kelsey took a quick look over her shoulder at the disconsolate Airedale and said, "Not today. Maybe we could detour by a pet store while we're in town. There are a few things I have to buy."

What with the rehearsal deadline and the shopping expedition, lunch had to be at a coffee shop instead of the newest *creperie* near the town square that Norman had favored. He didn't hide his displeasure, even though it didn't spoil his appetite for a hamburger and french fries.

When they reached the pet store, it was discovered that Daisy had been chewing on the leather leash which Kelsey had left in the bottom of the car. Since the car upholstery was also leather, Norman made a point of saying he'd stay with the dog to make sure that she didn't start gnawing on the back seat.

Kelsey couldn't refute his logic but she did resent the way he was making a major issue out of it. He didn't need to act as if Daisy was going to start demolishing his car bite by bite.

By the time Kelsey finished her shopping list, she had an armful of parcels and her bank account was considerably slimmer. Norman had to open the car trunk to store the biggest package and the surprise on his face as he hoisted it in made Kelsey smother a chuckle.

"It's a sponge-rubber dog bed," she told him, getting her voice under control. "I had to buy the biggest one they made."

"When I grew up, dogs slept on the floor."

"They still do. This is just in case Daisy is tempted by a davenport. The furniture belongs to

43

Lucius and I'd like to have it in decent condition when he returns."

Norman made a derisive mutter as he waited for a break in the traffic and then pulled out from the curb. "You should let Brent worry about that. After all, it *is* his dog. Isn't it?" The last two words were tacked on suspiciously.

"Very much so," Kelsey said, thankful when they finally emerged from the city streets and headed toward the highway. "He's going to be well aware of it when I give him the bills. It must be cheaper to keep a mistress."

"Why don't you ask him and find out?" Norman slanted a secret smile her way as he accelerated up the hillside road. "But then Geraldine's an emancipated woman—so maybe he gets off easy."

If Norman had taken half the day to think about it, he couldn't have said anything to make Kelsey feel worse right then. She had often brooded about Geraldine's infatuation with Brent but she'd discovered that her feelings became still more intense when the woman was at close range. Even the thought of Brent taking the brunette out to dinner was enough to make Kelsey's hastily swallowed lunch feel like lead in her middle.

"It's a damned shame that you can't come to rehearsal with me," Norman was going on. "I could have used your help on proofreading the program notes. What about bringing them over to you later tonight?"

For the life of her, Kelsey couldn't think of a plausible reason why he shouldn't drop in. Especially since he'd made a habit of it in the past and usually she'd welcomed his company.

"That should be all right," she agreed, trying to sound more enthusiastic than she felt. "Maybe you'd better call first, though—just to be sure."

"I hope you don't plan to get Brent's okay." He was accelerating up the winding road faster than usual. Daisy tried to keep her balance on the back seat but she slid onto the floor with a thump when Norman braked abruptly at the freeway entrance.

Kelsey leaned over to assist the dog back onto her perch. "It's all right, girl, we'll be home soon."

"Sorry." Norman didn't sound apologetic and his next words proved it. "I'm not used to playing chauffeur for one of Brent's brainstorms. He just bought that dog to get some sympathy from you."

"That's absurd! He didn't even know that I was still at the house—and he certainly wasn't thrilled to find me there. Which made it unanimous," she added somewhat bitterly, staring out over the vast acres of juniper and piñon pine which comprised most of the scenery as they sped along the freeway.

There was heavy traffic from the north and Norman had to wait before he could finally turn onto the gravel road with its ditchlike arroyos which led to Lucius's neighborhood. Kelsey was more conscious than ever of the solitude and quiet as they drove along the winding track where homesteads were hidden behind adobe and shrubbery walls. Their residents had adhered to Santa Fe's historical building code, for the most part, with traditional low, sprawling styles. A few of the homes boasted tiled roofs but most favored the flat pitch to blend with a

45

stucco exterior, colored to resemble the old adobe dwellings. The architectural ploy succeeded very well—providing a beauty and seclusion for residents, like the land itself.

"That's what I mean," Norman burst out, startling Kelsey because her thoughts had been so far away. "You're different already. Didn't Russ's death mean anything to you?"

"That's a despicable thing to say!" She turned on the seat to face him, her eyes stormy. "Brent didn't have anything to do with the accident. He was with me when it happened—as you know very well."

"You weren't so charitable toward him later on. Or maybe time has dulled your sense of loyalty."

Her anger faded but he seemed almost like a stranger when she stared at his profile. "Loyalty is important to you, isn't it? I remember how you mentioned that word over and over at the time."

"Because you were getting a short shrift from Brent and his bunch of bloody bureaucrats. They couldn't find anything decent to say about Russ in their 'official' comments."

"I still think he was innocent and apparently you do, too. Maybe the rest don't matter. But let's not talk about loyalty anymore."

"I'm sorry . . ."

"Are you?" She faced him squarely on the seat as he slowed to turn into the driveway and braked in front of the house. "Then why did you bring the subject up again?"

"Because you can't keep closing your eyes forever to the fact that Brent Spencer doesn't give a damn about your family's reputation. No matter what you think, he doesn't walk on water and he can't . . ."

"You've made your point, Norman," she cut in firmly when he paused to take a breath. "Over and over again. Let's drop the subject—that's all I ask." She leaned back to slide a leather choke collar onto the dog who was pawing impatiently at the window. "And as for you, Daisy—simmer down. You aren't going anyplace except in the house."

Norman slid out from under the wheel and walked around the car to help. "My God, she's strong," he muttered as Kelsey pulled Daisy to heel with an effort. "I hope you shut her up somewhere when I come by tonight."

Kelsey saw no point in trying to evade the issue. "Don't count on it. Maybe in a day or two, things will settle down."

"What about dinner?"

She looked blank. "What about it?"

He shrugged. "I hoped we could have it together."

Kelsey found her key finally and unlocked the door, pushing the dog ahead of her into the house before turning back to Norman. "Let's skip dinner this time. It's going to take a while for Daisy's beauty session and by the time I finish with her— there won't be time for me."

"I'll still bring the program notes by," Norman insisted stubbornly.

"Whatever you say. You can admire my handiwork at the same time."

He raised his eyebrows disdainfully. "Dog grooming is hardly my line of country."

Kelsey battened down on her annoyance as she started to close the door. "Then I won't put you on my mailing list if I go into business. Would you please leave my packages on the porch—I have to take her into the utility room." He nodded curtly and turned toward the car, pausing only when she added, "Oh, Norman, I forgot to thank you for lunch."

"The less said about that—the better," he said as he opened the trunk and started dragging her purchases out.

Kelsey hesitated for a minute longer, then sighed and left him to it.

It took an hour and a half to complete the transformation on Daisy. The terrier was still a reluctant captive on the grooming table in the utility room when Kelsey finally refastened her collar. "It's just a pity we don't have a full-length mirror," she told the Airedale as she let her down from the table, "because you are simply gorgeous. Maybe a little overweight but who cares about that? Everybody's going to be looking at those legs and splendid chin whiskers now that we've combed them." Kelsey rubbed her own nose reflectively, trying not to sneeze as Daisy stirred some fallen locks on the floor. She urged the dog ahead of her. "Let's go out to the kitchen and raid the refrigerator to celebrate."

Daisy was enthusiastic about the idea. She was also enthusiastic about the cheese and crackers that were her first course. Afterward she sat by the refrigerator and waited for more largesse to fall on the linoleum in front of her black nose. "Now look," Kelsey said finally, "crackers have calories and your hips don't need any more of those. How about a carrot instead?"

Daisy nosed the first chunk cautiously but indicated that she'd go along with that, too. Carrots, a cabbage leaf, a sip of milk—all went down with enthusiasm. Kelsey suspected if she'd poured some of her tea in the plastic dog dish it would have been inhaled as well. "That's enough," she said finally. "This is just teatime. Dinner comes later."

After that, it took quite a while to sweep the utility room and dismantle the grooming paraphernalia. By the time everything had been put away, Daisy indicated a walk was next on the agenda.

Kelsey had forgotten how vigorous a walk could be, especially when towed by a big dog intent on investigating half the neighborhood. She was panting almost as hard as Daisy when they finally came back to the driveway, barely able to say, "Next time you take off after a rabbit—have the decency to bark first. I'll need another shower to get the pine needles out of my hair and you didn't do your looks any good either."

Daisy turned a deaf ear to the chastisement, only waiting for the door to be unlocked and her leash unsnapped before heading toward the kitchen.

Kelsey looked after her with a crooked smile. There was purpose in the dog's demeanor as she trotted away. Her chin was up, the soulful look was gone from the brown eyes—Daisy was now a force to be reckoned with.

There was barely time for Kelsey to wash her hands and run a comb through her hair when she heard the front door close again. Brent must be back, she thought, trying to ignore the way her pulse leaped. She schooled her reflection in the mirror as she heard him call her name, and walked out in the hall to tell him she was home.

He surveyed her calmly as he turned from the front closet. "Where's the pooch? Did you leave her downtown to get gussied . . ." The sound of paws scrabbling on the linoleum made him break off and peer around the kitchen archway. He braced himself as two unladylike paws came up to his chest, almost shoving him into the wall. "Good Lord! You mean this is Daisy!" He fended off the enthusiastic dog, reaching down to pat her rough head once the Airedale was back on the floor. "It's a blooming miracle. Did you do it all by yourself, Kelsey?"

His enthusiasm was so wholehearted that she sank down on a stool by the breakfast bar as a pleased reaction swept over her. To be in Brent's good graces again was a heady change and far more potent than she'd remembered.

"Daisy's ancestry deserves the credit," she said, trying to sound casual. "All I did was polish the rough spots."

"And get rid of a ton of hair. It's made all the difference." He didn't wince as Daisy dried her chin whiskers on his trousers before she flopped on the floor and closed her eyes.

"It's been a long day," Kelsey interpreted.

"So I gather." Brent brushed at his trousers. "It's a good thing I planned to change, anyway. I'm beginning to sympathize with Norman." He led the way toward a compact bar in the corner of the living room. "Let's let sleeping dogs lie. How about a drink?"

"Aren't you going out?" Kelsey moved to the end of a davenport and hovered there uncertainly.

He didn't turn around as he reached in the small refrigerator for ice. "There's enough time. Geraldine's coming to pick me up. That car of mine needs something drastic done to its insides. Do you want the usual?"

His quick change of subject was almost too much for Kelsey. She hesitated an instant before replying. "You mean tonic water?"

"And a small twist of lime."

"Yes, please." She sank onto the edge of the beige sofa. "I'm surprised you remembered."

His glance was hooded as he raised his head. "You'd be surprised at the things I remember."

Kelsey bit her lip, wishing to heaven that she hadn't let the incautious words slip out. She'd resolved to keep things light and businesslike between them while they were together—only to make a slip right off the bat.

Apparently Brent didn't want to linger on the past either because he said matter-of-factly, "There's another thing—I don't see any need for your changing bedrooms. I've thought about it and it'll be a lot easier if I just take the guest room and bath."

"It's no trouble . . ." she began but broke off when he shook his head decisively. "All right, whatever you decide."

"Then that's settled." He fixed his own drink and brought hers across in his other hand. After he gave it to her, he checked his watch. "If you'll excuse me—I'll get changed. Will you be all right tonight?" As she stared up at him, his voice took on an impatient edge. "You have enough stuff in the house for dinner?"

"Oh, that. Yes, thanks." She gave him a crooked smile. "Besides, Daisy and I could always eat out."

"Just so you remember that you're going steady with her. That was our agreement." He moved on over to the hallway, but lingered in the archway. "I can't think Norman would go for another date complete with chaperone."

Kelsey's feminine pride roused itself. "Maybe he thinks I'm worth the bother."

"It's a possibility." Brent appeared to consider it and then shrugged. "To each his own—or words to that effect. Is there enough hot water for a shower or did Daisy deplete the supply?"

Which showed how much he cared, Kelsey thought, annoyed. "There should be plenty but I'd like to take a bath myself in a few minutes."

"Good luck." He raised his glass in a sardonic toast and turned down the hall, leaving her to stare irritably after him.

The movement roused Daisy from her nap. She struggled to her feet, yawned hugely, and walked over to the big living-room window, putting up her nose to investigate the glass. Discovering that it held no future for her, she moved over to the open glass door and went out to flop on the surface of the deck. Kelsey stood up and followed, leaning against the sliding door to stare out at the deserted landscape. A minute later, she frowned as she realized that the peaceful surroundings weren't working their usual miracle; her thoughts were staying annoyingly close to home.

Apparently the skirmishing had begun and so far Brent was way ahead on points. She'd have to rethink her strategy—that was clear.

She pushed away from the doorway with an abrupt movement, and started for the hallway herself. Halfway across the living room, she stopped. Then she moved purposefully across to the bar and found a bottle of gin on the counter. Splashing a healthy measure into her plain tonic water, she took a tentative sip. She almost choked but grimly stirred it with her finger and then carried the glass to her bedroom.

A little later, she discovered that she'd have to rethink her strategy in a tubful of cool water since Brent had apparently copped all of the hot. She took another sip of her gin and tonic as she stood and watched the tub fill. The alcohol didn't do a thing to help dull the pain, she discovered, but at least it might help to keep her warm.

Chapter 3

ACTUALLY, it was the sound of rain on the skylight a little later which prompted Kelsey to get out of the bath more quickly than she'd intended. During the past month, experience with sudden New Mexico downpours made her give them due respect. That open glass door onto the deck could cause trouble if the wind was blowing the wrong way, and it was too much to expect that Daisy would pull it closed with her teeth.

Probably it was more likely that she'd still be out in the rain, which meant that Kelsey would have to mop up more than the floor.

She hurriedly toweled herself and reached for her blue-and-white sprigged robe. The house was quiet except for the rain on the roof, indicating that Brent had gone on his way. It flashed through her mind that he could have at least knocked on the door to say he was leaving but she dismissed the idea impatiently. After all, she was only in the house on sufferance. Her lips quirked at the thought—sufferance was certainly the operative word.

The noise of rain on the flat roof was even more pronounced as she went into the hallway and she didn't waste any time heading for the living room, the long skirt of her robe billowing behind her. She was so intent on her task that she was almost halfway across the thick carpet before she absorbed the fact that the glass door was already closed and the rain she could see bouncing on the deck was safely contained.

Her body sagged with relief, only to become poker stiff as Brent drawled from the bar at the corner of the room, "You didn't have to worry—Daisy gave the alarm."

Kelsey clutched the edges of her robe, attempting to cinch up her belt. "I should have known," she managed to say. "What did she do? Ask you to turn off the rain and push the sunshine button again?"

"More or less." Brent put away the gin bottle with more emphasis than necessary, letting Kelsey know that her maneuver for Dutch courage hadn't gone unnoticed. "You feeling all right?"

Just as if she was weaving around and had to hang onto the edge of the davenport, Kelsey thought rebelliously. She drew her hand back as if the upholstery had suddenly become red hot. "I'm fine. I thought you'd gone."

"I gathered that. Geraldine hasn't shown yet. Time doesn't mean much to her."

"Amazing. She's so efficient in other ways."

"Isn't she?" Brent's tone matched hers for silkiness. "But then she's worth waiting for."

A noise from the kitchen made Kelsey's head turn. "Daisy can't be eating again?"

" 'Fraid so." Brent's expression turned rueful. "She invited her chum in out of the rain and one thing led to another."

Curiosity overcame Kelsey's determination to remain aloof. She moved over to the kitchen doorway and found Daisy whiskers deep in a dish of dry dog biscuits. Above her, on the kitchen counter, Elmo munched solidly on the same product from a cereal bowl. "Good Lord," Kelsey murmured, astounded.

"You'd better do some more shopping tomorrow. Elmo has trouble chewing the bigger pieces."

"Your grocery bill is going to be like the national debt," Kelsey warned, amazed that a man who looked as handsome as Brent did at that moment could be discussing dog food. His light gray suit emphasized the breadth of his shoulders and the pale blue of his shirt provided striking contrast with his tanned skin. It would have made more sense if he'd been lounging against a bar in Monte Carlo instead of scratching the ears of a scruffy tomcat in Santa Fe.

Evidently such thoughts never crossed Brent's mind. All he said was, "We'll survive. After some of the food bills I paid abroad, this won't make a dent."

"I hope you feel the same way after feeding Geraldine tonight," Kelsey informed him. "Some of the restaurants around here have copied their European cousins."

"If I get what I hope, it's worth any price." The expression on her face made him add irritably, "Oh, for God's sake, Kelsey, pull that mind of yours together! Do you honestly think that I'd be standing here bragging about making out on a date—like some teenager trying to impress his buddies!"

"It's none of my business what you do—"

He broke in curtly. "It's conceivable that you

56

might show a legitimate interest. Nothing's really changed between us. You'd better grow up and acknowledge it."

"You're a fine one to talk! Waltzing in here and making a dinner date with Geraldine the first time you get a chance."

"Only because she claims to have some new information about Russ's accident." Brent's words cut across her indignation like cold steel. "I didn't want to say anything until I had something definite but . . ." His shrug was as graphic as any words could have been.

"Did she tell you what made her suspicious?" Kelsey asked eagerly. "She must have names or evidence. Otherwise she wouldn't have mentioned it."

"When I learn anything definite, I'll let you know. Can't you trust me that far?"

Kelsey bit her lip, knowing how she must have sounded. "I'm sorry. It was just hearing there might be some hope after all this time." She had to swallow before she could continue. "I do trust you, Brent. Does this mean that clearing Russ's name is the reason you came back?"

"One of the reasons." Brent didn't linger on the topic. "Most people would say I was overdue. Anyhow, Geraldine should be here anytime."

"If you want to borrow my car, rather than having to use hers, it's all right with me. I don't plan on going out," Kelsey confessed. If it would help unearth any facts in Russ's tragic death, Brent could have anything he needed. Within reason, of course. Her hands went up to again tighten the belt on her thin robe as his considering glance swept over her.

What he saw seemed to amuse him. "You mean that you've ditched Norman for the time being?"

"Well, he's planning to drop by a little later on," Kelsey admitted, annoyed to find that she was on the defensive again.

"Then you'd better get dressed, hadn't you?"

"I *am* dressed." Her hand swept down in a gesture that encompassed the floor-length of her robe. "There's certainly nothing wrong with this."

"Except that you don't have anything on underneath. You didn't use to be quite so informal, as I remember." He shoved his hands in his pockets as he stood by the fireplace.

Her color rose as she confronted him. "I just came out to close the window, so you needn't be so damned stuffy. As I remember," she quoted him deliberately, "you didn't used to be."

"I've changed. You've given me good reason to," he informed her, taking the offensive with a vengeance. "Exactly how much does your pal Norman know?"

Kelsey's hands clenched at her sides but she kept them hidden in the folds of her robe. "What do you mean by that?"

"Stop stalling—we don't have all night! I want to know what you've told him."

"About your coming back?" She shrugged. "Just the bare bones. That Lucius invited you to take over."

"And before that?"

"Nothing special," she flared. "He doesn't ask a lot of questions; he was just there when I needed him."

"If you hadn't been so quick to come up with all

the wrong answers and then leave town—you wouldn't have had to depend on Norman." Brent reached up and rubbed the back of his neck. "Just make sure that you keep the status quo."

"You'd better explain that."

"Oh, for God's sake, Kelsey—do I have to spell it out?" His words came out like chips of ice. "Keep your lap dog around if you must but don't be handing out any tidbits."

Her chin tilted defiantly. "I was wrong. You haven't changed at all. I hope you use a different technique with Geraldine tonight. You'd better, unless you want to walk home."

The sound of a horn from the driveway cut into her last words and Daisy set up a crescendo of barking in the kitchen intermingled with a distinct thud. Brent strode over to the doorway and peered in.

"Elmo's dish took the count. Unfortunately, it landed in the middle of Daisy's water bowl, so I'd suggest a mop." He moved leisurely toward the front door. "I may be late—don't feel that you have to wait up."

His parting remark didn't improve Kelsey's humor, nor did her peek through the kitchen window which revealed Geraldine in a stunning burnt-orange creation. Kelsey glanced instinctively down at her robe, knowing that Brent wouldn't miss the difference either.

Daisy nuzzled her at that point, startling Kelsey so that she stepped into the spilled water on the linoleum. "I should make you do the mopping," she admonished the big dog as cold water lapped around her toes. "Along with your chintzy feline friend." She looked around and sighed. "Who managed to get out while he had the chance."

The sound of Geraldine's departing car prompted Kelsey into getting dressed first. She didn't have any intention of receiving Norman the way she was, so Brent hadn't needed to lecture her. It had been sheer perversity on her part not to admit it.

She changed into an apricot shirtwaist which still looked crisp after she'd mopped the puddle from Daisy's water dish. The big Airedale sat watching with her head cocked, clearly fascinated by the goings on.

Norman, arriving a few minutes later, found the two of them still in the kitchen about to enjoy some onion dip on crackers. Kelsey warned him about the damp linoleum when he crossed the threshold.

"You mean that Brent actually told you to mop the floor?" he asked.

"Well, I didn't *have* to," Kelsey admitted, beginning to find the humor in the situation, "but it was a little soggy otherwise. Especially since I planned to invite you to dinner."

"I suppose that means you aren't free to go out."

Kelsey started to laugh. "You don't do much for a woman's ego, Norman. I'm not *cordon bleu* but I never had *that* reaction to a dinner invitation before."

He gestured apologetically. "I didn't mean it that way. Maybe it's just as well if we stay in. These program changes have to get to the printer tomorrow." As he put them on the counter, he noticed Daisy's new profile. "That's quite a transformation. How about working on her manners next?"

"One thing at a time—right now I'm concentrating on yours," she said frankly. "You're like a different person today—what's come over you?"

"I should think it would be evident. First you welcome back the man who labeled your stepbrother a thief. Then you calmly hire yourself out as a dog-sitter to a canine pachyderm. And you wonder why I'm unhappy."

"Are you finished?" Kelsey asked.

Norman couldn't miss the dangerous tone in her voice. He grimaced and would have put his arm around her except that Daisy rose to her hind legs between them at that moment and he staggered under her weight.

Kelsey tried to keep a straight face as Norman fended off the dog. "Daisy, behave yourself! Come along," she said, taking hold of her collar. "There's a splendid bed waiting for you in the other room. You can have a nap while I fix dinner. *My* dinner," she emphasized as the brown eyes looked up at her hopefully. "You've had yours. Come on now—I'll let you out in a little while."

Norman brightened perceptibly when Kelsey returned unencumbered. "You've parked her?" he wanted to know.

"At least until I can broil our steaks. Want to fix a drink while you're waiting?"

"You bet. You're finally sounding like my girl." Norman headed toward the bar in the living room. "The rest of this day has been like a bad dream." He surveyed the bottles in front of him. "Tonic or a martini?"

"Nothing, thanks. I had something earlier." She was investigating the contents of the refrigerator, emerging with lettuce and a cucumber which she put on the counter.

"You mean with Brent?"

"That's right," she reached in the refrigerator again and came out with two plastic-wrapped steaks. She waved them suggestively at him. "And unless you'd want to wear one of these rather than eat it—we'll change the subject."

He came back to the kitchen, drink in hand. "Just because I show a normal reaction when another man muscles into my territory?"

Kelsey was honestly perplexed. "I didn't realize you felt that way, Norman. We've been friends for such a long time . . ." Her voice trailed off helplessly.

He put his glass on the countertop and came over to shake her gently, nuzzling her cheek afterward. "You should know by now that a man doesn't hang around for months just for friendship."

"You never mentioned anything else."

"Because I like to choose my time. You haven't been in the mood to discuss a permanent relationship." He gave her a reassuring squeeze before going back to perch on a stool. "Actually I hadn't planned to say anything now but Brent's arrival changed everything."

Kelsey remained outwardly calm but she was wishing to heaven that they'd lit on another subject for discussion. She stood on tiptoe to get a wooden salad bowl, saying, "That's absurd and you know it. Why, you've always had a string of girlfriends on both coasts."

"I didn't want to rush you."

"Heavens, I didn't mean it that way." Kelsey wasted no time in setting the record straight. "I thoroughly approved."

"That isn't very flattering." A woeful expression came over his face, making him appear more vulnerable than usual. "Probably I shouldn't have said anything tonight—you're tired after wrestling with that dog all day."

"I'll recover fast once these steaks are ready," Kelsey said, keeping a careful watch on the broiler.

"Don't you have *any* romance in your soul?" Norman slammed his glass down on the copper tile. "I've practically proposed and all you can talk about is what we're going to eat."

"Considering the price of steak these days, you can't blame me." She relented as she saw he was serious. "I *did* try to head you off. Right now, I don't want any more complications in my life."

"What about later?"

Kelsey chose her words carefully. "It wouldn't work, Norman. I think you know it, too. Besides, there's another reason that I'd rather not . . ."

"Why don't you just admit that Brent has you wrapped for delivery whenever he's in the neighborhood." Norman took a swallow of his drink and went on before she could interrupt. "Well, go ahead and play house with him for a week or two if that makes you feel better, but don't make any long-range plans. Not with Geraldine quitting her job."

63

"The altitude here has gone to your head," Kelsey said, sliding out the rack to turn the steaks. "I'm not playing house with anybody and Geraldine didn't say anything to me about leaving town."

"I said she was quitting," Norman announced, his tone showing his triumph. "That doesn't necessarily mean leaving town. Why should she? Brent's just come back."

Kelsey kept her face averted as she placed the broiler tongs on the edge of the sink. Norman's announcement wasn't completely convincing but even the possibility that he was right made her queasy. "Where did you get all this information?"

"At the Opera House this afternoon." He stuck out his chin when Kelsey turned to frown disbelievingly. "I mean it. Some people were talking."

"I didn't know Geraldine had any friends down there."

"That's because you haven't circulated much since you've come back. She's one of the volunteers—tours people around backstage on weekends during the season."

"Have you run into her?"

He poked one of the ice cubes in his drink with his finger. "I've talked with her a couple of times."

"It's strange you didn't mention it."

"You weren't here at the time." Taking a final swallow of his drink, he moved over to put the empty glass in the sink. "Can I do anything to help?"

"The silver's in that drawer beside you," Kelsey said, slicing cucumber into the salad bowl. "You'll find place mats in the drawer below." As anxious as

64

she was to change the subject from Brent's secretary, Norman's announcement had sidetracked her, leaving her thoughts almost as mixed as the salad in the monkey pod bowl. "I shouldn't have thought you would find much to discuss with Geraldine. Last year, you were blaming her even more than Brent."

"People change," Norman replied, folding paper napkins as carefully as finest damask. "Why don't you ask Brent about her finer points when he comes back tonight? He's an expert in that line."

"They're only on a dinner date—not some clandestine weekend," Kelsey said, reaching over to switch off the broiler and haul out the steaks. "You've been watching too many soap operas."

"Have it your way but I can't see Geraldine giving up her career at Los Alamos without a good reason."

"Well, I doubt if it's Brent."

"Why not? Why can't he latch onto her?"

"Because I think he has—" Kelsey hesitated before finishing weakly, "I mean, he *had* commitments."

When it was clear that she wasn't going to say any more, Norman uttered a muffled expletive. "Don't dish it out like the salad, for God's sake. What kind of commitments? You didn't make a complete fool of yourself this morning, did you?"

"I'm going steady with an Airedale at the moment." She gestured toward the plate in front of him. "And if you don't eat that steak while it's hot—that Airedale's going to get it."

Norman looked as if he wanted to pursue the subject but the sizzling steak made him decide to satisfy another hunger first.

After the steak and salad, there was lemon custard pie topped with whipped cream. By the time Norman had settled onto the big davenport in the living room with a cup of coffee, Kelsey had successfully diverted the conversation toward the program notes he'd brought.

"These look good to me," she said after reading the copy. "I think that revision on the apprentice program at the Opera House helps." She got up from the davenport. "Half a minute and I'll be back."

"Where are you going now?"

"I want to check the dog. It's entirely too quiet in the utility room," she said, starting toward the hall.

"What's wrong with that?"

"Nothing except I don't trust her—she might have chewed her way through the back door by this time."

"If that's the case, just let her go."

Kelsey shot him a speaking look over her shoulder and disappeared down the hallway. In a very short time she was back with the dog, keeping a firm hand on her collar. "Lie down there in front of the fireplace," she told Daisy. "I intend to keep an eye on you."

"What's the matter?" Norman inquired laconically. "Couldn't she manage the door?"

Kelsey shook her head. "She was too busy shredding a straw bag that I bought in Baja."

"Probably sulking because she missed out on the steak."

"Who knows? I think she's still suffering from jet lag." Kelsey watched the dog settle by the hearth before she picked up the program notes again. "Are you taking these to the printer tomorrow?"

Norman nodded as he shifted on the couch to face her. "I'll have to if we make the deadline. Unless there's a really gross error . . ."

". . . leave them alone," Kelsey finished for him. She shrugged as she handed back the pages a little later. "Everything looks all right. They'll give you a chance to see final proofs, won't they?"

"I'll make sure they do," Norman promised. "This benefit means a lot to me. If I show the visiting brass that I can handle organization on a big production, it could give me an entree to some of the Coast shows. Maybe even Broadway. I'm sick of little-theater stuff all the time."

"I didn't realize that it was so important to you," Kelsey said. "You've always seemed contented with your lot—especially here in Santa Fe."

"With a few low-budget commercials on local television?" Norman leaned forward to put his empty coffee cup on the low table in front of him. "I must be a better actor than I thought."

"Well, you don't really need the money."

"An inheritance doesn't rule out a man's ambition. My God, who wants to play in the bush leagues forever? I know I don't." He made a wry face. "Sorry, I didn't mean to sound like the lead in that melodrama downtown. And after you fed me, too."

She made an effort to match his change of mood. "You're right. Complaints go with hamburger. Steak rates . . ."

". . . soft music and a different dialogue. Usually staged with two people on a sofa. Two people alone."

His expression hardened as Daisy stretched out and noisily started licking a paw. "You'll notice that Brent didn't take that oversized dustmop on *his* dinner date." At that moment Daisy tired of her paw, getting up to pad over to Kelsey's side. Norman bounced to his feet as she approached. "Hell, I might as well go! She'd probably take a hunk out of me if I laid a finger on you."

He seemed determined to be as sarcastic as possible, Kelsey decided. There wasn't much chance of altering his mood under the circumstances and, if the truth be known, she was too tired to struggle. "You may have a point, there. By tomorrow her disposition should have improved. Daisy! Get down! Don't jump on people!" Kelsey's last admonition came when Norman attempted to bestow a casual kiss as she walked with him to the door. "I'm sorry, Norman," she added, hastily opening it so he could escape. "At least her paws aren't muddy."

"I *had* noticed," he said bitterly. He lingered on the porch as Kelsey kept a firm grip on the dog's collar. "Tell Brent when he comes in that he won this time."

"I don't even expect to see him until morning."

He shrugged. "No matter." He jerked a thumb toward the station wagon pulled over to the side of the drive. "For a minute, I thought he'd come back early."

"No. They went in Geraldine's car tonight."

"He must really have the whammy on her. She's spent most of the day driving him around and picking up his livestock."

The same thought had occurred to Kelsey but

she'd chosen not to dwell on it. "I'll probably talk to you tomorrow or the next day," she said, changing the subject determinedly. "Good luck at the rehearsals!"

"We need it," Norman replied and opened his car door. "Let me know if you want to attend one of them and I'll tell the guard at the gate. Don't forget, there are no dogs allowed."

Kelsey managed to keep a pleasant expression on her face as she waved and watched him drive off but she had no sooner closed the door than she told Daisy, "If you were hoping to collect a brass ring from Norman—you just lost. I must say, though, that you're terrific as a chaperone. It almost makes up for your treatment of my straw bag. And leave that cup alone!" The last came when the rubbery black nose investigated the dregs of Norman's coffee on the table. "Come on," Kelsey added in resignation as she picked up the leather leash, "once more around the park and then we're both going to bed. It's a pity that washing dishes isn't one of your talents," she added as she stooped to fasten the clasp. "Well, Brent will just have to find them stacked by the sink—for tonight, at least. Although it will probably be so late when he gets back . . ." Her voice broke unhappily as she thought about it. With uncanny instinct Daisy chose that moment to lick Kelsey's cheek. Kelsey drew back but smoothed the Airedale's whiskers before getting to her feet again. "For that, *enfant terrible*, you may get the bone from that left-over pot roast a little sooner than I planned."

Daisy's deportment was beyond reproach after that. When they returned from the walk, she went meekly to her foam-rubber bed. Kelsey had prudently moved it into her own bedroom to avoid a chance encounter with Brent if the dog started wandering or barking in the middle of the night. She'd already discovered that Daisy's "woofs" were uttered in an unladylike bass and had tremendous carrying power.

Fortunately the cat wasn't around to rouse her and the dog settled down easily. Kelsey read for a while, unconsciously listening for Brent's return and then, realizing what she was doing—turned out her light in disgust.

She lay back but knew that sleep was going to prove elusive. The pale moonlight that filtered in the window cast shadows on the bedroom carpet, making a pattern as complex as her thoughts. In the corner of the room by the empty beehive fireplace Daisy shifted in her bed and emitted a gusty sigh, as if giving thanks that the light had finally been extinguished. Suddenly the eerie howl of a predator echoed mournfully through the night air outside, making the dog stir restlessly before she settled down again. Kelsey's own reaction was quite different; it wasn't the four-footed predators bothering her just then. Far from it! It was in the middle of that profound thought that exhaustion overcame her and her eyelids stayed down.

Even so, her rest was disturbed. She couldn't sort out the sequence of events afterward but she was groggily aware of Daisy's presence in the room. The first time the dog started to pad about, Kelsey muttered, "Lie down, that's a good girl," and promptly went back to sleep again. When she heard a sharp "woof" and the scrabble of Daisy's paws on the floor by the window later in the night, Kelsey surfaced only enough to utter a protesting groan.

It was considerably later that the situation became reversed. A thin "wowrr" barely penetrated the bedroom's walls, but it brought Kelsey upright like a fire alarm erupting in her ear. "Oh, damn!" she muttered and pushed the covers back, searching for her slippers as soon as her feet touched the carpet. She started to reach for the switch on her bed lamp and then stopped. If she could leave the bedroom without awakening the dog it would certainly be a step in the right direction.

She didn't linger to put her robe over her thin pajamas, but tiptoed to the door and managed to get out into the hallway as Daisy shifted in her bed. An instant later Kelsey closed the door just before a demanding paw raked the other side.

Kelsey ignored it and went down the hallway, detouring by the moonlit kitchen to rummage beneath the sink. Then she moved determinedly into the living room where a scurrying and rustling could be heard. She reached over and switched on a table lamp, having a very good idea of what the light was going to reveal.

Her past experience was right on target; the illumination showed a familiar feline figure crouched intently at the edge of the drapes.

"Elmo—I'd like to wring your neck," Kelsey whispered as she advanced cautiously. "Where have you got him this time?"

Elmo showed disdain for an uninvited player in his game by keeping his attention glued on the drapery. An instant later, he stretched upward in a lightning gesture as the fabric quivered.

"Get down from there!" Kelsey ordered him just as quickly. "You know what happens if you climb around on those." She dropped what she was carrying and pounced on the tomcat, managing to catch him while his attention was diverted. Clutching the back of his neck, Kelsey carried his squirming body to the hall closet and closed the door on him. She hesitated then, helpless between the cat's howls of protest from the closet and Daisy's rising crescendo of barks from the bedroom. Since there wasn't anything she could do about them at the moment, Kelsey hurried back to the living room and searched the drape where Elmo had centered his activities. "I thought so," she murmured an instant later and retrieved the paper bag she'd brought from the kitchen. She put it carefully beside the drape before picking up the other bit of kitchen paraphernalia she'd collected. Just then a masculine voice interrupted the proceedings.

"What in bloody hell is going on?"

Kelsey gave a startled look over her shoulder to see Brent glaring at her from the hall. Wearing just a robe thrown over his pajama bottoms, he was braced against the archway, trying to hang onto Daisy's excited form.

"You *do* know what time it is?" he went on grimly.

"I don't care what time it is," Kelsey said. "Get her out of here or you'll ruin everything."

"It was to keep the bedroom door from being splintered that I brought her along in the first place.

72

What in the devil are you doing with those kitchen tongs in your hand?"

"I am trying to catch a mouse," she began through clenched teeth. "If you and Daisy will let me."

His eyebrows shot up. "With a pair of tongs?" As the Airedale scrabbled on the slate, trying to get in the fray, he said over the din, "Stay right there. I'll put Daisy back in the bedroom."

Kelsey watched him disappear and then, shaking her head, approached her task again.

Brent came back into the room just in time to find her depositing a very small mouse, clutched firmly by the metal tongs, into the paper bag.

"You mean there *was* a mouse all the time?" Brent asked, raking a hand through his tousled hair.

"Naturally." Kelsey kept her voice calm although her fingers were trembling as they quickly folded the top of the grocery bag. "It's Vincent again."

"Vincent?" Brent barely breathed the word. He made an obvious effort to collect himself. "You mean you have a pet mouse, too? What is this—a damned zoo!"

"He's not my mouse. He's Elmo's." Kelsey kept her clutch on the bag so that at least one thing was under control.

"Elmo?" There was a distinct pause. Then, carefully, "You mean he's back, too?"

"Of course. He started the whole thing. It's the third time this week that he's brought Vincent with him."

Brent chewed on his lower lip, trying to phrase his next question without offending her obviously

73

disturbed mind. "How do you know it's the same mouse?"

"Because he only has one ear and there can't be that many idiotic one-eared mice in this place. Every time it's the same thing—I have to catch him and take him out again. You'd think he'd have sense enough to leave the neighborhood while he's ahead."

Brent put one hand to his head, looking as if he'd like to clutch it. "Why Vincent? No—don't tell me. Van Gogh, of course."

"Naturally. Although if he hangs around with Elmo much longer, he'll be missing more than an ear."

"I could suggest a permanent cure right now," Brent offered, his manner back to normal.

She drew herself up, unconsciously projecting a delectable figure in sheer batiste attire. "No way. I'll take him out to the driveway again. Don't let Elmo out of the closet until I get back."

Brent shuddered at the sounds coming from behind the door. "I wouldn't get within arm's reach of that cat when he's in a good mood—let alone now."

"Well, he'll just have to find something else to occupy his time from now on."

Brent eyed the paper bag which was also giving off sounds of agitation. "Vincent evidently feels the same way. I suggest you let him hit the road before he chews through that thing."

"Oh, Lord! I forgot about that possibility." She started for the front door. "Usually I don't waste any time transferring him outside."

"What are you going to do with those tongs?"

"Put them back under the sink when I'm finished." She shot him a puzzled glance over her shoulder and then smiled as his query registered. "Why? Did you think I was going to put them back with the kitchen cutlery?"

Brent's slanted grin showed that he'd been caught but he simply waved her on. When she returned, he was still leaning against the living-room archway. In the meantime, he'd tightened the belt on his robe but that was his only concession to formality.

Kelsey knew that her own outfit was lacking a few requisites, as well. The drafts were whipping around her bare ankles and Brent's encompassing regard as she checked the chain lock on the door made her wish fervently that she'd put on her robe before dashing out of the bedroom. She managed to retain a modicum of poise, however, as she walked over and opened the closet door, catching Elmo in the act of sharpening his claws on it. Recovering quickly, he stalked into the hallway with a glance that should have shriveled anything in his path.

Kelsey wasn't impressed. "It serves you right," she told him as he lingered to lick his paw. "Next time, I'll keep Vincent and boot you out into the cold."

Elmo bestowed a glassy stare and stalked toward the utility room, his tail twitching.

"You made a great impression," Brent said dryly after watching the exodus.

"I can tell." Kelsey sighed and closed the closet door. "I'm sorry that you were disturbed. Actually I hadn't realized you were back."

The grandfather clock in the hall chimed three at that moment and Brent jerked his head toward it.

"I've been back to hear it chime midnight and all the rest. Plus Daisy's outburst about one-thirty." When Kelsey looked puzzled, he persisted, "My Lord, I didn't think anybody could sleep through that!"

"I'm just programmed to wake up when Elmo plays tag with Vincent. You'll have to give me another day to fit Daisy into the schedule."

"Well, if this is a sample of the nights around here, I can understand why you looked tired today." Brent bent to switch off the living-room lamp before rejoining her in the hall.

Kelsey bit her bottom lip in exasperation. To think she'd been worrying about her lack of attire and all Brent had noticed was the circles under her eyes. "It's been a busy summer," she said to cover the silence. "That's why I was looking forward to a vacation."

"And instead you find yourself ringmaster for a menagerie." He gestured her down the hall ahead of him. "At least you can save rent money for a while —but maybe that isn't a problem for you."

She pulled up in front of her bedroom door, trying to decide whether his remark had the undertones of a dirty crack or whether she was being unduly sensitive. "I still come out right with my checkbook at the end of the month."

"So I understand—you'll have to tell me sometime how you've managed so well." When she opened her mouth to reply, he shook his head. "I'd rather wait until daylight for the confessional. There's an early meeting tomorrow, and if I don't get some sleep, I won't have much to contribute. Unless you've changed your mind, I'll borrow your car in the morning to drive to Los Alamos and then take mine to the garage in Santa Fe when I come back. The way the engine sounds—that's about as far as it'll go." When she hesitated, his mouth firmed into a grimmer line. "Naturally I'll reimburse you for any inconvenience."

"I was just trying to remember what I'd planned for tomorrow morning," she said hastily, "but you're welcome to the car. My extra keys are on a hook by the front door."

Brent's frown eased. "Fair enough. I'll leave my extra ignition key on the counter in the kitchen. The station wagon should be all right for a short errand but don't try a cross-country run."

"You won't have to worry. It wasn't on my schedule."

"I'm glad to hear it." He reached out to restrain her hand on the bedroom doorknob. "If I remember, though, you make up your mind in a hurry. That's what you said the other time, but the next thing I knew you were on your way to the East Coast."

Her hand tightened on the doorknob under his grasp but there was no way for her to get through the doorway without pushing his solid frame aside. About as easy as raising the *Titanic*, she decided, eyeing his broad shoulder wedged against the doorjamb. She could only pray that he didn't hear her heartbeat thudding like a long-distance runner's as he lingered just a whisper away. "I thought you didn't want to drag this out," she protested.

"I have no intention of it," he said. "Mine was a

simple observation so there's no need for you to get so upset."

"I'm not upset—I'm just tired."

"Oh?" Kelsey tried to appear just as dispassionate under his level gaze but she knew she wasn't fooling anybody. The concrete proof came an instant later when he said, "Then why is your pulse racing a mile a minute?"

She wrestled her hand away with an angry gesture. "I don't have to stand here and answer idiotic questions. I *told* you that this arrangement would never work. Now that Geraldine is quitting her job, you can get her to 'house-sit' or 'dog-sit' or whatever you call it."

"Geraldine has other things to do." His gaze wandered over her angry flushed face. "I see the native tomtoms have been at work. Your friend Norman must get around."

"So does Geraldine," she mocked even as she noted that he hadn't denied her accusation. "It makes no difference to me, one way or another."

Brent reached out then, with such an abrupt gesture that she had no way of avoiding the lightning movement. It wasn't until she felt a tug on the gold chain around her neck that she guessed his motives.

"Leave that alone!" she gasped, trying to wrest it from his fingers.

"Stop it or you'll break the chain," he told her, keeping a firm grip on the diamond ring that hung like a pendant from it. "So this is where it's been all these months. I'm surprised that Norman didn't convince you to trade it in on something more practical."

"You needn't be insulting . . ."

"I'm just being practical." He held the ring carelessly on his forefinger. "Most women would either wear it or get rid of it altogether. But maybe you're still trying to make up your mind. That's one of your problems, Kelsey," he added conversationally, just as if they were holding an abstract discussion in the living room instead of sandwiched against a doorway in the middle of the night. "You lack the courage of your convictions."

She drew herself up stiffly. "What *is* this fascination with my failings? Do you fancy yourself as Torquemada these days?"

His eyes narrowed and he used the fine gold chain to pull her even closer. "This is hardly an inquisition—just a few home truths."

Kelsey drew a deep, ragged breath. She had to, even though she knew that the movement was a dead giveaway to her agitated state. Since she was keeping her glance lowered, she saw that Brent's chest was moving with calm regularity under his robe—showing that propinquity was only working one way. There was a time, she thought despairingly, when things would have been different. The memory brought a bitter undertone to her voice as she said, "If you don't mind, I'd prefer to go to bed." When there was only silence, she glanced up to see his mocking smile. "Alone," she added pointedly.

"Oh, I'm sure of that." He let her feel his fingers against the soft skin between her breasts as he deposited the ring carefully back where he'd found it. But it seemed that he wasn't through tormenting her because an instant later those same fingers caught her chin, lifting it so that she was forced to meet his gaze. "I wonder if you could be persuaded to change your mind?"

His voice was gentle and deep, his gaze almost mesmerizing. Despite herself, Kelsey yielded to the hard masculine arm that moved down to her hips, molding her body to his. The fresh lemony tang of his after-shave triggered even more familiar memories, and as his head bent over hers she relaxed in his unyielding embrace.

Just one kiss couldn't matter, she thought, knowing that logic had nothing to do with it. More than anything else, she wanted to feel Brent's lips on hers again. It was the only thing she'd *really* wanted ever since he'd walked through the front door that morning.

She drew a deep breath and emitted a slow, satisfied sigh as she closed her eyes, just waiting for Brent's mouth to cover hers.

As the moment stretched unconscionably, even her addled mind realized that something was wrong. Her eyelids went up again and she beheld Brent's motionless countenance, still inches away. As she stared, he released her. "The defense rests," he said dispassionately, and walked down the hall toward his bedroom without looking back.

Chapter 4

MORNING seemed to take forever to arrive.

It wasn't surprising, Kelsey thought as she turned restlessly on her bed. She'd heard every chime of the clock since she'd parted from Brent and managed to collect a miserable headache in the bargain. The headache was an unwelcome aftermath of the tears of frustration that she'd shed, recalling the way Brent had humiliated her.

When dawn finally made itself known, Kelsey stayed motionless with her eyes closed. She didn't stir when she heard Daisy being quietly summoned for an early walk, nor later when noise from the kitchen showed that Brent was fixing breakfast. Since the sounds were muffled, Kelsey presumed that he had no more desire to renew their acquaintance than she did.

Not that he had any real reason to postpone the encounter. He'd left the battlefield the night before with the war won. Not only had he routed the enemy, but he knew with a certainty that any victory spoils could have been his without effort.

Kelsey, on the other hand, had to face the bright light of day acknowledging that she'd abandoned her pride, and gone down to an inglorious defeat of her own making. It was enough to make any woman's head ache!

Finally there came a whine from the dog as she was presumably incarcerated in the utility room and the welcome sound of Brent's footsteps going down the hall for the final time. The front door closed and, a minute or so later, a car started in the driveway.

And it was *her* car, she recalled belatedly, which added insult to injury. She got out of bed and padded to the bathroom to take some aspirin for her headache before donning a robe and going down to let Daisy out of her holding cell.

The Airedale wagged her tail but headed for her foam couch in the bedroom, curling into it with a determination which told Kelsey that breakfast was going to be a solitary affair.

Not only that, it was going to be short-lived, Kelsey discovered when she opened the refrigerator door a few minutes later. Brent must have used the last drop of milk. She couldn't face eggs so early, which left a limited selection of toast and coffee—black coffee. Daisy's dish in the corner still bore a few milky traces, and she looked at it longingly. No wonder the dog had settled back into bed with every evidence of enjoyment. She and Brent apparently had consumed a full-course breakfast.

There was no point in sitting around brooding about it, Kelsey decided. As soon as she got dressed, she could make a quick trip down to the neighborhood grocery near the highway and restock the larder. Brent had assured her that his station wagon would be serviceable for a short jaunt.

The Airedale opened her eyes as Kelsey went back into the bedroom but closed them again and settled even more comfortably into the foam mattress while Kelsey donned a denim skirt and plaid cotton shirt in shades of blue.

Kelsey slipped into a pair of denim espadrilles and picked up her purse, before eyeing Daisy's recumbent figure. "If you'll promise not to gnaw on the dining-room table while I'm gone, you can stay here."

Two brown eyes stared up at her even as the brown whiskers remained firmly on the edge of the mattress.

"I won't be long," Kelsey assured her. "For heaven's sake—behave yourself while I'm gone."

Kelsey gave herself a mental shake afterward as she collected Brent's car keys and let herself out of the house. It was absurd to feel uneasy over leaving the animal alone for a short time! Daisy would probably be sleeping soundly when she returned.

The engine of the station wagon sounded asthmatic but it caught on the third try. Kelsey nursed it carefully and let it run for a minute before heading out the driveway. The motor was still missing on some cylinders when she reached the gravel intersection, and since there was no traffic in sight she turned onto Tano Road without hesitating.

Probably she should have let the engine warm up more, Kelsey thought as she drove along the winding track. Then the noise coming from under the hood suddenly sounded more reassuring and Kelsey pressed down on the accelerator. Everything was going to be all right, after all. It was a good thing because Tano

Road was apparently deserted again. Sometimes she wondered if the other residents ever emerged from their elegant dwellings.

Normally Kelsey enjoyed the feeling of isolation as she drove through the unadorned stretch of juniper and piñon at either side of the road but she realized that it could be a lengthy wait if Brent's engine conked out that morning. The possibility made her bear down more heavily on the accelerator as the station wagon left a ridge and started down the incline on the other side. There was a sharp turn at the bottom of the hill and she automatically braked on the familiar approach. An instant later, her knuckles went white on the steering wheel when the brake pedal flattened against the floorboard under her foot. The station wagon hurtled unchecked into the curve, even as Kelsey fumbled for the emergency brake. She stamped on it just as the car careened into the sharp curve. Probably she could have controlled it if the wheels hadn't hit a layer of loose gravel that repair crews had left after filling some potholes. The station wagon fishtailed in the fine rock, and even as Kelsey fought to control the spin, skidded sideways into a two-foot drainage ditch at the edge of the road.

Her seat belt held Kelsey behind the steering column as the wagon finally jolted to a stop in a screech of metal and breaking glass.

For an instant she was unable to move, shocked by what had happened. Then, sanity returned and she realized that, other than still shaking like an aspen, she had apparently escaped unharmed. It must have been the headlights she'd heard breaking, she thought as she stared blankly through the still-intact windshield. Lord knows what the paint on the side of the car looked like. And what would she tell Brent!

The smell of dust filtering in the window made her realize abruptly that there wasn't any gasoline odor along with it. Thank God for extra favors, she thought, even as she reached for the handle and struggled to push open the heavy door. There didn't seem to be any spilled fuel, but she'd better get out first and investigate from a safe distance.

A second later, pain streaked through her ankle as she tried to lever herself upward. Kelsey winced and sank back on the seat again, aware that she hadn't come through the experience unscathed. Then she bit down hard on her lip and managed to slither off the vinyl car seat through the open door. She tried to avoid putting any weight on her wrenched ankle in reaching the ground, but lost her balance in the attempt and collapsed in an inglorious heap on the gravel shoulder just as she heard an approaching car.

It ground to a halt in the middle of the road while she was still trying to push herself upright and she recognized the brown leather loafers and blue-jeaned legs even before Brent spoke.

"Stay right there!" he commanded, sounding more terse than she'd ever heard him. "Let me find out if you've broken anything."

She tried to steady her labored breathing. "That won't be hard. At least two fenders and most of your paint job bit the dust."

"The hell with the car!"

"My feelings exactly. I don't think much of your merchandise." She tried to keep her voice steady while he ran his hands over her but couldn't restrain a quiver as he checked her rib cage.

"Does that hurt?" he wanted to know, frowning in concentration.

"A little," she lied frantically, hoping he'd move his fingers before he became aware of what his touch was doing to her. "Actually, you're in the wrong hemisphere. It's my ankle. The right one," she added as his disturbing hands slid obediently downward. "I must have twisted it when I tried to brake."

"Why in the devil were you going that fast in the first place?" His tone was considerably more concerned than critical, despite his words. "Does it hurt when I do this?" he continued, pressing her instep without giving her a chance to defend herself.

"Not too much. It's just when you waggle it from side to side. Like that," she added with a gasp.

"It's probably a sprain," he said, lowering her foot carefully again, "but there's no point in taking chances. I'll drive you down to town for an X-ray." He pulled a clean handkerchief from his pocket and gently flicked grit from the knee she'd scraped getting out of the car. "Do you want to go straight away or would you rather detour by the house?"

"And clean off the topsoil?" She took a deep, shaky breath and nodded. "I certainly need to do that first. Can I hitch a ride with you?"

"I sure as hell didn't plan to leave you here by the side of the road. From what I've seen, there might be another car along in a day or so." He pulled her up beside him and then easily swung her into his arms.

86

Kelsey remained as stiff as possible until he deposited her on the passenger seat of her own car a minute later. Then she felt obligated to ask, "What about your car? We can't just go off and leave it here."

Brent looked over his shoulder. Then he straightened, and went across to take the keys from the ignition of the wrecked station wagon. "It'll take a tow truck to get it out of that ditch," he remarked as he came back and slid behind the wheel next to Kelsey. "Here—let me help you with that." The last came as he reached across and slammed the door at her side. His arm brushed the front of her shirt in the process and she gave a faint startled gasp. If Brent heard her, he didn't let on. An instant later he started the car.

The silence lengthened between them as he drove carefully back over the road she'd covered only a few minutes before. In the narrow confines of the front seat, she was more aware than ever of his tall masculine frame—even of his shoulder muscles and strong tanned arms in the short-sleeved shirt he was wearing. Her thought processes still weren't functioning at normal capacity but the incongruity of his attire did register and make her say accusingly, "I thought you had a meeting first thing this morning."

"Was that what inspired you to drive flat out to town?" He didn't give her a chance to deny it before he went on. "There *was* a meeting. I simply called them from Santa Fe and told them I couldn't make it."

Kelsey felt an irresistible urge to quarrel with him. It might have been reaction setting in or just recalling his behavior from the night before. Whatever the cause, he wasn't going to get the upper hand again. "What's wrong with the telephone at the house?"

"Not a thing when I left. I had to go into town for some milk, so I used the phone there when I was at the store."

His matter-of-fact logic didn't help Kelsey's mood. Especially when he added comfortingly, "You'll feel better after that ankle's strapped."

"I feel perfectly fine right now . . ." she countered fiercely and then sank back on the seat. "Who am I kidding? I wish I'd known that you were bringing the milk."

"You mean that's why you were tearing into town?"

"I wasn't doing anything of the sort. I wasn't going any faster than you are right now. Or, at least, not much." She raised her chin defiantly. "You could have told me about the brakes."

His eyebrows drew together. "What in the devil are you talking about?"

"I'm not just talking—I'm complaining. Why didn't you mention that your brakes were bad?"

Brent let up on the accelerator as he shot a quick look at her. "You mean it?"

"I don't joke about going in the ditch. What does it take to convince you, for heaven's sake?"

He grimaced apologetically, pulling over to the side on the deserted road and letting the engine idle. "Let's get this straight. Tell me exactly what happened."

"It won't take long." She took a deep breath. "I

admit that I was going a little fast to make the corner when I came down the hill, but when I put my foot on the brake pedal, it went flat to the floor. It all happened so quickly." She rubbed her forehead as she tried to remember. "I'm not sure whether I ever did find the emergency brake. Once I hit that loose gravel, the ditch came right up to meet me."

Brent's expression was ominous as he glanced in the rear-view mirror and then pulled slowly out onto the road again. "I can't blame you for being mad. The thing is—I didn't warn you about the brakes because there wasn't a damn thing wrong with them yesterday. The engine almost conked out on me but that was all."

"Then something's rotten somewhere and not only in Denmark."

"That makes two of us with the same idea. After we get back to the house, I'll alert the foreman at the garage. Once they've towed it in, we should know more."

"I hope so." She pushed a strand of hair back from her cheek with a nervous gesture as he slowed to pull into the drive in front of the house. "Either I had too much coffee this morning or not enough. Right now, I feel like I'm missing some cylinders, too."

"You'll be better in a few minutes. It's amazing what soap and hot water can accomplish." He looked around the quiet forecourt as he braked and turned off the ignition. "Is the pooch still inside?"

Kelsey nodded. "She was sticking to her bed when I left. Apparently she didn't like being parked in the utility room."

Brent grinned as he came around to open the door on her side. "Daisy's catching on to her new surroundings entirely too fast. Don't put your weight on that ankle—put your arms around my neck so I can carry you."

"There's no need—I can walk—" She broke off as she was hoisted in his arms without any more discussion.

"If you want to be helpful, get your key out and unlock the door," he instructed as he stopped in front of it. When she had the key in her hand he bent forward easily so that she could insert it, and straightened after she'd opened the door.

Daisy started barking as soon as they went in the house. "Brace yourself," Kelsey murmured, hearing the scrabble of paws on slate down the hall.

Brent deposited her hastily on her feet but had her shored against his side by the time the big Airedale appeared. "Get down, you idiot!" he commanded, trying to fend off the ecstatic welcome. "Let's face it, you're not a lap dog."

"Don't hurt her feelings—she's only a little overweight," Kelsey cut in, patting the rough head.

"I was referring to the breed, not her waistline. Although that could stand some whittling, too. Her current motto must be 'If you can't be the best—be the biggest.' " He steered Kelsey down the hall toward her bathroom, letting Daisy bring up the rear of the procession. "Can you manage this clean-up by yourself or do you need help?"

"I'll be fine, thanks," she said hastily once they reached her door. "You must have other things to do this morning. Honestly, there's no need whatsoever for you to stick around—" She broke off abruptly when Brent placed a firm forefinger over her lips.

"You do have a tendency to run on. That's another thing I've remembered." He opened the door and gestured her into the bathroom. "Sit down on the edge of the tub while I get some antiseptic."

"I *told* you—I can manage . . ." Her voice wasn't as firm as it might have been because her ankle was aching badly. When Brent placed an authoritative hand on her shoulder, she sank onto the edge of the tub without protesting further.

For such a large man, he was extraordinarily gentle as he washed the grit from her knee and palms. "The highway-maintenance department will complain if you make a habit of this," he said with a grin when he put the basin aside and started to dry her skin. "Abrasions can hurt like the very devil, though. Make sure the doctor looks at them as well as your ankle."

"I refuse to have a trauma about a skinned knee. You should have seen me in third grade—that was the year I took up roller skating."

Brent had just put the antiseptic back on the shelf of the medicine closet when the doorbell set Daisy barking again. "Ah, right on time," he said in a satisfied tone.

"You're expecting company?"

"A friend of mine. I called her from town this morning," he replied, hurriedly rinsing his hands.

"I wish you'd stop talking in riddles," Kelsey muttered, beset with a sinking feeling in her middle. Apparently Brent's circle of female acquaintances in the neighborhood knew no bounds.

"Just sit still, you can meet her a little later. My God, it sounds as if Daisy's clawing that door to pieces." Brent barely bothered with a backward look as he disappeared into the hall.

"Exactly what I'd like to do," Kelsey muttered darkly as she struggled to her feet. She had no intention of languishing in rumpled clothes if still another of Brent's *innamorata* had come calling. Working like a quick-change artist, she'd just finished getting into clean jeans to hide the scrapes on her knee when Brent pounded on the bedroom door.

"Are you all right in there?"

"Fine—I'll be out in a minute," Kelsey called back, her fingers hastily buttoning on a patchwork shirt.

"Give a shout when you're ready."

Kelsey's brows came together over that remark. Tucking in her shirt, she made her way to the door and pulled it open. "Why should I do that?" she asked, stopping Brent halfway down the hall.

"I was going to help you out to the kitchen," he said, coming back. "You shouldn't be walking around on that ankle."

"Well, I'm not going to sit around with my foot on a cushion," she said, using the wall for a brace as she started toward the living room. "I thought you had company."

Without ceremony, he reached down to swing her into his arms. "Don't you ever do what you're told?"

"It depends." Kelsey had trouble sounding annoyed because it was considerably less painful in his arms than struggling to proclaim her independence.

And there wasn't time for another argument just

then because a short, gray-haired woman bustled in from the kitchen to supervise as Brent deposited Kelsey on the living-room davenport.

The newcomer was wearing a print caftan which couldn't disguise the fact that there was a great deal of poundage underneath its generous lines. She had a plump face to match but just then its serenity was upset by Kelsey's plight. "You poor lamb," she said, visibly concerned. "Brent told me what happened to you. It's a mercy that you weren't hurt worse."

"Kelsey, this is Mrs. Foley who's the regular housekeeper for Lucius when he's home," Brent said. "She's very kindly offered to come and help us out now."

"To tell you the truth, I've been bored just sitting home all summer," the older woman said. "Anything more than a two-week vacation isn't much of a treat for me." She reached down and fondled Daisy's ears when the Airedale emerged from the kitchen to see what was going on.

"I hope you like dogs, Mrs. Foley," Kelsey said, still dazed at this latest acquisition.

"Sakes alive, I was practically raised with a Great Dane—this one looks small by comparison," the older woman said, beaming. "And just call me Vera—it's what I'm used to. Come on, Daisy, let's dry your whiskers on a paper towel before you drip over the upholstery."

Brent had an amused look on his face as he watched the two of them go back into the kitchen, but it disappeared when he turned to Kelsey. "Are you ready for that X-ray? The clinic can fit you in whenever you appear."

"I guess so. If you really think it's necessary. Do you have time to take me?"

"You need a lot of convincing. What do you think I'm waiting around for?"

"I didn't know." She turned up her palms in a helpless gesture. "I thought maybe Mrs. Foley—I mean Vera—was going to do it."

"Vera will hold the fort. And the dog," he added before she could ask. "Since you're not going to be available for long walks in the immediate future, it's a damned good thing." He walked across the hallway to the closet and pulled his poplin jacket from a hanger. "You'd better have a sweater or something, too. We can stay downtown for lunch after you check with the clinic. How about this?" he asked, as he searched through the clothes on the rack and emerged with her short white leather jacket.

By then, Kelsey was regretting her decision to appear in jeans and the comfortable but hardly glamorous patchwork shirt. She could at least have put on her new beige corduroy pants that fit like a dream. Turning her head, she saw Brent staring at her impatiently. "I beg your pardon," she said, wondering what she'd done wrong this time.

"Do you go into a brown study every time you get ready to leave?" As she frowned, he said, "'The jacket. Remember?"

"Oh, that." She limped over to take it from him. "It'll be fine. We can pick up a hamburger at the drive-in," she added, letting him know that she didn't expect an expense-account lunch just because he'd had a kindly impulse.

"You've become remarkably frugal in the last few months. Is that why Norman sticks so close?"

"Certainly not. He has some sort of inheritance, I think. Not that I've ever asked him."

"Such tact and virtue," he mocked, standing by the front door. "It's enough to make a man suspicious."

Kelsey managed an uncaring smile even though his jibe hurt. "I'll be just a minute—I want to tell Vera something."

"Go ahead." He started back down the hall toward his bedroom. "There's another phone call I should make. I'll meet you in the car."

Probably he wanted to let Geraldine know of his latest change of plans, Kelsey thought rebelliously as she headed toward the kitchen. The sight of the dog helping Vera investigate the contents of the refrigerator was a welcome diversion. "I've learned one thing already," Kelsey told the housekeeper. "Daisy will spend the day there if you let her."

Vera patted her ample girth beneath the caftan's folds. "I can sympathize. The same thing appeals to me. Does a key lime pie sound good to you for dinner?"

"Heavenly—but you don't have to worry about food."

Vera smiled sunnily. "That's not on my list of troubles. You and Brent go ahead—I'll take care of things here. It seems good to get back to work."

"Well, in that case, you might have another mouth to feed. There's a cat by the name of Elmo who comes calling. The carton of liver by the freezing compartment is what he's after."

The older woman nodded. "That sounds simple enough. How does Daisy react?"

"At the moment she can't tell whether she loves him or hates him."

"Just like some couples I've met. Probably they'll end up sleeping in the same bed. Is there anything else I should know?" Vera asked, apparently amused by Kelsey's sudden surge of color.

"No—that's all." The younger woman put up her palms to cool her hot cheeks and then realized that she was under scrutiny. "I'll go on out to the car."

"Sure you don't need some help?"

"Positive." Kelsey gave her a wry look as she started out the door. "Believe it or not, there are a few things I still have under control."

Chapter 5

BRENT came out to slide beneath the steering wheel just a minute or so after she'd gotten settled in the front seat. "Sorry to keep you waiting. Wouldn't you be more comfortable in back with your foot up?"

"This will do nicely, thanks." She watched him nod and turn the ignition switch, pulling out into the curving drive with his usual economy of motion. They were on the main gravel road to the highway before she added, "I feel guilty about taking up so much of your time, though. Won't you get in trouble at work?"

"I doubt it."

He kept his voice solemn but she could tell that it was an effort. Color surged to her face again as she recalled that engineering-project supervisors didn't punch time clocks or have to account for every minute away from the office.

"I have some leave coming," he explained, making her feel better. "Probably I would have played hookey anyhow—you've just given me a legitimate excuse. Did you get things settled with Vera?"

Kelsey nodded, saying, "She's a pearl beyond

price—even Daisy thinks so. I can see why Lucius keeps her on salary while he's away." She shifted on the seat so that she could watch his profile more easily. "Actually, now that she's come, you won't need me anymore. As soon as I can find a room, I'll be on my way."

"Why?"

The terse monosyllable made her eyes widen. "What do you mean?"

"Exactly that. There's no reason for you to hare off just because Vera's arrived to spell you in the dog-sitting department. She still likes to go home at night." He flashed a sideways glance, letting her see the cold expression that rarely left his face when they were together. "Don't tell me that the night shift has you worried? I didn't lay a finger on you, if you'll remember."

"That wasn't what I . . ."

"Maybe I should change that to *more* than a finger," he amended, interrupting her ruthlessly. "Is that what's bothering you? You don't look as if you slept very well."

"The main thing that's bothering me right now is my ankle," she snapped. "You try sharing a room with an Airedale and you'll miss some sleep, too." She crossed her fingers as she spoke, sending a silent apology to Daisy who had scarcely stirred during those hours. It was either that or let Brent know that his actions had left her an emotional basket case. Somehow she felt that Daisy would approve.

"In that case, you'd better move her bed into my room and see if you can do better."

There was no doubt about it, Kelsey thought disconsolately, she should have worn something else. Or maybe it wouldn't have done any good since Brent practically had her wrapped in a shroud anyhow.

A thick silence fell between them for the next mile or so. The formidable line of Brent's jaw showed that *he* wasn't in the mood for polite conversation and Kelsey's pride kept her from discussing the weather or the scenery. On the other hand, it seemed infantile to ride all the way to Santa Fe in silence.

Fortunately, the sight of Brent's car still resting in the ditch provided a neutral subject. He slowed to edge past it, mentioning casually, "The garage said that they'd send a tow truck out right away."

"It hasn't really been long." Kelsey twisted in her seat to confirm that she really *had* made a mess of the station wagon's front fender and probably the rear one, as well. "I feel terrible about it."

"If the brakes were gone, there wasn't a damn thing you could do," Brent said, accelerating again once they'd turned a corner and the wagon was out of sight. "The garage promised a report as soon as they get it in the shop. With any luck, we should know by the time you're finished at the clinic." As they rounded another curve and he saw a tow truck speeding toward them, he gave a throaty murmur of satisfaction. "Raise the flag! They're actually on the way."

"Do you want to go back and oversee things?"

Brent shook his head, pulling over to the side of the narrow road so that the speeding tow truck had plenty of room to pass. "I'd hate to meet him on a curve," he muttered. "It's a good thing there isn't much traffic."

"That's an understatement. Before you came along, I felt as if I were in the middle of Death Valley."

"That's not surprising, considering the circumstances."

Kelsey stared at his profile in surprise. If she hadn't known better she would have thought that he was tossing out a few olive branches himself. Her fingers went to her throat in an unconscious gesture but she no sooner touched the gold chain which was hidden under the vee neckline of her shirt than she stiffened and hastily brought her hand back down to her lap. The ring she was wearing on the chain had caused enough embarrassment last night—it was the last thing she wanted mentioned just then.

If Brent had noticed her movement, he was kind enough to ignore it. Or maybe he had decided that a rough gravel road under the New Mexico sun wasn't the proper stage for ultimatums or declarations.

That thought triggered another in Kelsey's mind. "If you're serious about lunch, I really should tell Norman about it."

"Why? I'm not inviting him."

"You know what I mean," she countered impatiently. "He'll probably phone me this morning."

"In that case, Vera will tell him that you're out." He braked before turning onto the north-south highway which skirted Santa Fe and accelerated to freeway speed.

Within ten minutes they were in the center of town and drawing up before the clinic, which like everything else in the city had two faces. Outwardly it reflected the traditional style of the Southwest, appearing to be constructed from the mud, straw, sand, and water which comprised original adobe. A closer look showed that it was merely stucco covering the integral frame. Since the stucco had been colored to match the truly old structures and the exterior *vigas* or beams showed a careful patina of age, the clinic blended into the block as if it had been there since the Confederacy.

"Want me to hold your hand?" Brent asked as he pulled up in front of the emergency entrance.

"If you did, they'd send me to an analyst instead of X-ray," Kelsey retorted, trying to sound as if she could hardly wait to march through the clinic's doors.

She must have been more successful than she imagined because when he came around to her side of the car and opened the door, he simply said, "O.K.—if you're sure. Where shall I meet you?"

"You won't want to wait around here," Kelsey said as an orderly hurried past with a wheelchair for some unfortunate soul in the van which had just pulled up behind them. "How about under the portal at the Palace of the Governors on the plaza? I should be finished here in an hour. Give or take a few minutes," she added, remembering how medical appointments had a way of taking most of the forenoon.

Brent nodded and walked back around the car to the driver's side. "If you don't appear eventually, I'll come back here. Whatever you do, stick around until they read that X-ray."

The conscientious young doctor who attended

Kelsey in the emergency section thought her drawn countenance was due solely to her aching ankle, and it was simpler not to correct him. Kelsey *was* cheered when he reported considerably later that the X-ray had shown nothing broken.

"It's a nasty sprain, though," he said, waving her to an examination table so he could tape it. "Unfortunately, these things take a long while to heal. Taping it should give you added support for a day or so." When he'd finished and helped her to the floor again, he added, "Don't enter any marathons and keep your foot up whenever you have the chance. Is that clear?"

Kelsey thought about asking for a prescription that called for an immediate flight back to New York. Aloud, she merely said, "The bandaging helps already. Thank you for seeing me so promptly."

"Brent Spencer can be very persuasive." For an instant, the doctor's grin was unprofessional. "This time I understand why and you can tell him I said so. Give me a call if you have any problems."

"With the ankle or him?" The words were out before she knew it and his grin broadened.

As Kelsey left the clinic, she decided that her cheeks had been wearing a permanent flush for the past thirty-six hours. She should have lingered to inform the doctor that Brent's emotions had nothing to do with his arranging for an appointment; he would have been as conscientious with any wounded female in his care. And with most of them, he'd be waiting in the main hall or at least by the entrance door instead of picking them up later at the Plaza.

Kelsey didn't dwell on that discouraging fact, but

congratulated herself that her ankle in its firm taping felt much better. She experimented and found that if she stuck to level terrain and didn't try any soccer kicks that she was practically as good as new.

When she arrived at the portal of the Palace a few minutes later, brilliant sunshine was pouring down on the plaza. It added to the fiestalike atmosphere found among the native salespeople who represented many of the New Mexico Indian tribes and the throngs who strolled the length of the block seeking treasures and bargains in their displays.

It wasn't surprising that there was such an extensive selection because Santa Fe boasted more artists and craftsmen in residence than any other city in the United States. That morning the offerings were even more attractive than usual, Kelsey decided. She wandered in front of the wares where famed silver jewelry predominated as usual. The intricate workmanship included turquoise insets in most pieces, with coral mosaic a close second. Some vendors showed samples of pottery but they were the exceptions, most tribes choosing Santa Fe gift shops to sell the expensive ceramic pieces.

Kelsey had stopped in front of a modest jewelry display near the end of the block, admiring some coral ropes in variegated shades when she heard Brent's familiar voice behind her.

"It's a relief to see you're looking at jewelry," he said, moving to her side. "For a minute I thought you were in the market for one of those." He indicated a row of elegant silver tongs inlaid with turquoise.

Kelsey stared at them with a puzzled frown and

then started to laugh. "For Vincent, you mean? It's a thought. But have you looked at the price tag on those beauties?"

Brent bent over to check the figure and whistled softly. "I see what you mean. Would you settle for going out to lunch instead?"

Kelsey pretended to consider it and then nodded, allowing herself to be led across the picturesque plaza which marked the heart of Santa Fe.

There were other strolling couples on the crisscrossing paths of the plaza but not enough to disturb the town's sleepy atmosphere. Even two dogs investigating the shrubbery weren't taking their work very seriously.

Brent was watching Kelsey's progress, remarking after they'd gone a few feet, "The car's not far away. If you'd rather, I can come and pick you up. There are plenty of benches . . ." He broke off as she shook her head. "You feel okay, then?"

"Practically as good as new." She shot him an upward covert glance. "But that wasn't a question, was it?"

"I had a chance to check with the doctor," he admitted.

"For heaven's sake, don't you think I can be trusted. It *is* my ankle."

"Then you must be glad that there's nothing a little care and time won't put right," Brent said smoothly. "The car's on the other side of the street. I was lucky to find a place in the shade." He was steering her toward it as he spoke.

"But we're not eating downtown?" she asked.

Brent unlocked the car door and helped her in before he answered. "I thought that we might pick a place where it's cooler. How does a picnic sound?"

She stared up at him as he stood by the open car door, "Well, fine—but we'll have to go back to the house and get the food. Wouldn't it be easier just to stay there and eat on the deck?"

He grinned and closed the door, coming around to slide behind the wheel. "I thought a few honest-to-God trees and cool breezes sounded better. Besides, I've already taken care of the lunch. What did you think I was doing when you were at the clinic?"

A sense of anticipation made Kelsey's voice breathless. "Don't tell me you were whipping up sandwiches in the back seat?"

He flicked the end of her nose with a casual forefinger. "You must be feeling better—you're getting impudent again. Take my word for it, there's food in the back. We can go down Pecos River way, if that's all right with you." He turned on the ignition and started to pull out of the parking place before she could reply.

Kelsey didn't miss the fact. For an instant, she thought about announcing that she couldn't take time for a picnic—that a quick lunch in town was all she'd bargained for. It would certainly be an effective way of deflating his assurance and salvaging some remnants of her feminine pride.

On the other hand, if she turned down the picnic—she had a sneaking suspicion that she'd be eating a peanut butter sandwich at home with only Vera and Daisy for company.

"Or we could postpone it until another time . . ."

Brent's concerned words finally penetrated her

thoughts. "I beg your pardon?" she stammered, confused.

"You look as if your ankle's bothering you. Maybe a picnic isn't such a good idea."

"I think it sounds terrific!" Kelsey said impulsively and afterward mentally threw up her hands. Of course, she was going with him. The issue had never really been in doubt. "I was just thinking," she offered in a lame explanation.

"You don't have to worry about the car—if that's bothering you. I haven't left it untended long enough for anybody to try for a repeat performance." He managed a sidelong glance. "You were right about the brakes on the station wagon. The fellow at the garage said there wasn't any doubt that they'd been tampered with. Some wiseacre had cut nearly through the cable. All it took was one hard push on the pedal to completely sever it."

Kelsey had to swallow before she could reply. "And the brakes were all right yesterday so it must have been done sometime last night."

He nodded grimly. "All ready for me to drive to work this morning. By rights, your sprained ankle belongs to me." The last came in a lighter tone as he stopped at an intersection and then turned south.

"*Now* he tells me," she said, trying to match his mood. "Next time I lend you my car, I'll post a sign in the front yard."

They reached the edge of Santa Fe and Brent had increased his speed on a winding but almost deserted two-lane road before he broke the silence again.

"Was there any disturbance outside the house last night?"

Kelsey rubbed her temples, trying to think. "Not that I remember. Norman left fairly early."

"Why? Something go wrong?"

The underlying amusement in his tone brought her chin up fast. "Certainly not," she declared staunchly, if not quite truthfully. "He has a lot on his mind these days. The success of that benefit at the Opera House means everything to him. I really should have called him to say that I was going out today."

"He can't blame you for a change of plans. A sprained ankle wasn't in your schedule for the morning." Brent slowed behind a car which had signaled for a turn, and then accelerated smoothly.

He drove just the way he did everything else, Kelsey thought. With a minimum of effort and a maximum of efficiency. She knew that she was a good driver, yet Brent's touch far surpassed hers.

Another four or five miles went by before he interrupted her contemplation of the scenery. "You didn't mention to Norman that I was having car trouble, did you?"

"Not that I remember," Kelsey replied, pulling herself back from her daydreams reluctantly. Just then, it was enough to be sitting and admiring the peaceful beauty of the approaching mountains with Brent at her side. "I don't think we discussed you at all." Which wasn't exactly true but she had no intention of quoting Norman's feelings on that score. "What about Geraldine?" she said, going on the offensive.

Brent kept his attention on the road. "What about her? I can't see Geraldine down in the dirt disabling

107

my car. It would have been easier for her to simply run me down in the parking lot when we reached the restaurant last night."

"Very funny," Kelsey said in a prim tone. "It's different if it happens to be a friend of yours. Or maybe 'friend' isn't the right word."

"I'd hoped we could stow the accusations for an hour or two," Brent said, sounding as if he was thoroughly sick and tired of the subject.

"I wasn't accusing her. Geraldine isn't the type who'd recognize a wrench unless it was in with her lipstick. But she does have friends around town and I doubt if she kept your arrival a secret."

"Touché." Brent sketched a rough star on the windshield as he acknowledged her point. "So—unless you have a bunch of homicidal maniacs for neighbors, Norman and Geraldine are the prime suspects."

"The nearest neighbor is a sweet old lady of seventy-five who divides her time between watching birds on the deck and soap operas on television."

"Not exactly the type," Brent conceded.

"Hardly. Don't get the wrong idea, though. She's the best-adjusted person I've met in Santa Fe."

He grinned. "Maybe you'd better introduce me one of these days." Then, the grin faded, and he added, "So where are we?"

"I'd say about twenty miles from Santa Fe," she said, deciding there was no point in continuing such a depressing conversation. "And about twenty minutes from lunch. That's if you're going to the picnic ground I remember . . ." She broke off, bit-ing her lip. "I thought we were just getting out of town for a picnic in the woods, not raking up old memories."

"If it bothers you, we can certainly pick another place. One's as good as another as far as I'm concerned." As they passed a sign announcing a fish hatchery just ahead, he added, "How about stopping along here? We can have a nice erudite conversation on the merits of rainbow versus cutthroat trout during lunch." He slowed and gestured toward the hatchery lot at the side of the road. "Unfortunately, those are two school buses parked under the trees. That means sixty kids plus chaperones. How does that appeal to you?"

"Like a blizzard on the Fourth of July," she said through clenched teeth. It would serve him right if she called his bluff but she wasn't strong enough to battle the third grade en masse. "Drive on, you . . ."

"Fiend—bastard—cretin," he supplied helpfully.

"Any one will do."

"I don't know why you're so upset about going back to a picnic ground," he said matter-of-factly. "It's been more than a year since we were there. That's certainly long enough to lower the curtain on any memories, however distasteful."

Kelsey winced as if he'd struck her. So that was how he regarded the place where he'd asked her to marry him! And to think that all these months she'd kept that afternoon enshrined in her memory.

"Don't you agree?" he asked as they continued on the winding Pecos River road.

"Absolutely! On all counts," she assured him,

thankful that he couldn't read her mind just then. "It's nice that we both have an intelligent outlook." She gestured toward the rushing mountain stream just beyond the side of the road to emphasize her point. "One way or another—it's just water over the dam."

"Well, that should set a record for clichés, at least."

She chose to ignore that. "I'm only surprised that you didn't bring Geraldine here instead of me."

"What makes you think I haven't? You were away for a long time." He couldn't have missed her furious gasp but overrode it calmly. "Look, why don't you just settle down and admire the scenery? This was supposed to be a pleasant outing for you. We could have driven up the mountains beyond Los Alamos if I'd known this place bothered you."

"I'm just surprised by your choice, that's all. But then tact was never your strong point."

He kept his attention on the highway ahead. "I'd say it's a little late in the day to play the dewey-eyed maiden role about this place—considering what happened afterward. Even all the turmoil after Russ's death wasn't any excuse for taking off and leaving me flat."

Since there was a great deal of truth in his accusation, Kelsey had difficulty marshaling a defense. "It's easy for you to talk now. If you'd stayed around to help when it happened . . ."

"You weren't alone," he interrupted, his expression as glacial as his words. "You had Norman to hold your hand and pat you on the shoulder all that

110

next week. He even went East with you for the funeral."

"That's not surprising. He was Russ's best friend." Her chin went up. "There was nothing to stop you from joining us."

"I wasn't invited. By then, the two of you had drawn up sides and the fight was on."

"Only because you branded my brother a common thief."

"Stepbrother," he corrected.

She waved that aside. "Don't split hairs. You didn't wait for the investigation to be concluded or anything—you just smeared his name and didn't give a damn!"

"Kelsey, part of the documents he stole were still on the car seat beside him after the accident," Brent said, spelling it out.

"And the newspapers did the rest." She rubbed her fingers over her temple and then rested her head against the cool glass of the car window beside her. "Why did you have to bring it all up again?"

He pulled off the road into the graveled drive of a state recreational area and slammed on the brakes. "What in the devil am I supposed to do? Keep my head buried in the sand—the way you've done these past months?" He reached across and yanked the chain from the neckline of her blouse with a rough gesture. "That way you can wear this ring around your neck for the next fifty years like some flaky Victorian heroine." He dropped it back against her skin scornfully. "Maybe you should have seen a psychiatrist at that clinic this morning after all."

"If that's your opinion, you can have the ring

back," Kelsey said, trying to find the clasp on the chain so she could yank the diamond off. Naturally the damned clasp proved elusive and she wavered, wondering whether to break the chain to prove her point.

Brent clamped his hand over hers. "Don't try it or you'll be aching in more places than your ankle."

"I thought you were above that heavy-handed macho approach," she countered scornfully.

"It only comes out when I'm dealing with hysterical females." He took a deep breath. "Maybe we could try acting like responsible adults, at least until lunch is over?"

"Then take your hands off me." She waited for him to sit back behind the wheel before saying impulsively, "I would like to ask you one thing and then I promise not to mention the subject again."

"Fair enough. What's bothering you?"

"If you had it to do all over again . . ."

He didn't let her finish, interrupting to say grimly, "Would I act the same way? Is that what you want to know?"

She nodded, unable to hide the appeal in her glance as it held his.

"Exactly the same way." He didn't appear to find any enjoyment in his declaration but it wasn't any the less forceful for that. He put his hand on her thigh in a comforting gesture. "I'm sorry, Kelsey."

She took a deep breath and then opened the car door beside her, sliding out quickly so that he wouldn't know how his touch still made her quiver. "There's no need to be sorry." She flashed a bright meaningless smile in his direction as she stood by the open door. "At least now I know that I didn't do the wrong thing in running back to the East Coast all those months ago. My only mistake was in ever coming back."

Chapter 6

For a minute, Brent's expression was so ominous that Kelsey feared he'd simply drive off and leave her standing there. She remained frozen as his hands tightened on the wheel and he struggled to control his temper. Finally he slid out of the car saying, "At least we've got that out of our system. We might as well eat. From the looks of those clouds around the mountains, this sunshine won't last much longer." He opened the trunk and hauled out two cardboard boxes. "Can you get the thermos and those extra cups?"

Kelsey pulled herself together with an effort. "Of course. Anything else?"

"There's a blanket folded on the back seat. I'll take this plastic tarp in case any rain actually falls."

"I'd forgotten how quickly the temperature can change," she confessed once she'd gotten the blanket from the car and tucked it under her free arm. She moved automatically, trying not to show that her own personal private world had just come crashing around her ears moments before. "Probably it's because we're so high here."

Brent wasn't misled by her red herring. "Nice try,

114

honey. A discussion about the weather should safely get us to dessert and coffee, if that's what you have in mind."

That effectively dampened any more conversational attempts on Kelsey's part and she trailed him, squaw-fashion, along a dirt track which edged the bank next to the fast-flowing stream at their right.

There were mountains at either side of the narrow valley they'd been traversing—mountains that were mostly covered with greenery but still showed rugged stone slabs from an earlier geologic upheaval. The deep green of the vegetation contrasted dramatically with the blue sky and only the gray rain clouds clustering in the south neutralized the differences. The stream alongside the path was swift-moving and clear, faithfully reflecting the leafy tree branches which overhung the banks on either side. There were mammoth boulders in the water to change the course of the flow, and other smaller protruding rocks which merely added to the scenic beauty. At the bend of the stream up ahead a row of flat rocks had been arranged for a footbridge to the other bank.

She and Brent had used it that other afternoon, Kelsey recalled suddenly, and they'd gone barefooted because the current swirled over that third rock. It still did and her steps lagged because the memory of that enchanted interlude was so vivid.

Brent glanced back over his shoulder and pulled up. "Want to eat here?"

His prosaic question brought Kelsey swiftly back to reality. "It doesn't matter," she said with a careless gesture. "One place is as good as another."

He shrugged and put the lunch boxes on a flat rock

before spreading the plastic on a level grassy area at the top of the bank. After that, he took the blanket from her and spread it atop the tarp. Then he frowned as another thought occurred to him. "Maybe you'd do better sitting on a rock. That way you could stretch your ankle out in front of you."

She levered herself carefully down at the edge of the blanket before he could attempt to help her. "This is fine, thanks. I'll pour the coffee if you'll hand over that thermos." She was determined to get the atmosphere between them back to normal. Brent's behavior showed that he was hoping for a quick meal without any more emotional outbursts. The least she could do was oblige him.

When the coffee was poured, she opened the box that he'd put in front of her, trying to look as if food were the only thing on her mind.

"One roast beef and one turkey," Brent commented, keeping to his side of the blanket as he explored the interior of his own box. "Plus one dill pickle and two apples for dessert."

"We're almost a matched pair. Except that I have two chocolate-chip cookies for the last course," Kelsey said, unwrapping a sandwich.

He held out the two apples toward her, "Gentleman with a surplus of vitamin C desires to meet woman interested in acquiring same."

Kelsey pretended to consider as she took a bite of sandwich. "You'll have to do better than that."

"I'd settle for both cookies."

"No deal."

"You drive a hard bargain." He gravely handed over one apple and took a wrapped cookie in exchange. "The woman in the delicatessen got her signals mixed—I was supposed to get your box."

"If that's a sample of your negotiating, I hope you weren't handling any state secrets when you were in Europe. That is, if it was a business trip." He was unwrapping foil from his dill pickle, seemingly intent on the task and she added hurriedly, "Or should I ask questions about your job?"

He took a healthy bite of pickle and rested the remainder on the box within easy reach. "It doesn't matter these days. Solar energy is the division that wins friends and influences people. So long as you stay out of the Persian Gulf."

"I'll remember." She swallowed some coffee and then nibbled on a piece of turkey that had fallen on her napkin. "What made you switch to that field?"

"There were contributing factors. I thought it might be nice to sleep at night again."

She wasn't exactly sure what he meant but she didn't want to pursue it then. "More coffee?"

"When you fill yours. There's no hurry." He leaned back on an elbow and lifted his gaze to the mountaintops visible over the trees on the other side of the stream. "It's so quiet here. That came back to me when I was on a European picnic. But it wasn't only the scenery that seemed foreign over there."

"Go on," she urged when he paused. "You can't leave me dangling."

He took another swallow of his coffee and grinned wryly. "I discovered that I wasn't the 'loaf of bread, hunk of cheese, and jug of wine' type. It's strange what a difference little things make."

Kelsey wanted to ask if there had been a European

girl to help him with his research but didn't have the courage. She had to be satisfied with the surge of satisfaction she felt and say levelly, "I hope Daisy will transplant without too many traumas."

"We can always toss her a cucumber sandwich if she pines away. From the way she was inspecting the refrigerator with Vera this morning, I'd say she's already made the transition."

"I feel an awful fraud." When he shot her a puzzled look, she explained. "Letting Vera do all the work."

"Relax. After your experience with the car this morning, you deserve some rest and relaxation."

She smiled across at him. "Let's go back to discussing the weather. The thought of that severed brake cable doesn't help my digestion. Especially when we're not sure who it was intended for. This way, we both have to keep ducking."

"A very exclusive society," he acknowledged, "with a limited membership."

Kelsey started to take another bite of sandwich and then gave up, wrapping the remains neatly in plastic and putting them back in the box.

"You still have to eat lunch," Brent said, almost brusquely.

"I'll go on to the dessert course." Kelsey undid the plastic around the outsized chocolate-chip cookie and broke off a bite. "Ummm. That tastes good!"

The lines disappeared from Brent's forehead and he leaned back again. "If it makes you feel better, I'll even sacrifice mine to the cause."

She paused before taking another bite. "Now I *am* worried. Things have to be serious for an offer like that. Either that, or you want to accumulate some brownie points."

He raised an empty palm. "Nothing up my sleeve. What a suspicious nature you have, Grandma."

"With good reason. Don't forget, I've been picnicking here before." As soon as her snide comment was out she regretted it.

An angry color swept over his cheekbones. "Why didn't you tell me you were worried? I could have furnished shoulder pads and shin guards along with your coffee." He slammed the remnants of his own lunch back in the box and got to his feet. "We might as well start back to town if you're finished."

Kelsey nodded meekly, suspecting that even if she'd protested he would have gone without her. Her conscience pricked over her nasty rebuff but it was either that or confessing to Brent that being there with him again hurt far more than she'd dreamed it could.

She made a production out of emptying her coffee onto the ground while he waited impatiently to fold the tarp. Naturally the cup got cross-threaded on the top of the vacuum bottle when she put it away which took longer still. Kelsey, seeing the set of Brent's jaw as he waited, had to subdue an urge to giggle. If he'd had his way just then, it was obvious that he'd simply roll her in the tarp and sling her over his shoulder. "Just like Cleopatra," she murmured under her breath as she pushed awkwardly onto her knees.

"What's that?" Brent asked as he bent forward to help, pulling her upright like a cork from a bottle.

"Nothing," she said, swaying a little as she got vertical again.

He kept an iron clasp on her upper arm. "Are you all right?"

"Fine." She moved away to get what remained of the lunch. "This can be combined in one box and save space."

Brent folded the tarp with a few decisive moves and tucked it under his arm. "It doesn't matter—I'll dump it all in the litter can over there." He jerked his head toward the center of the picnic area where a brown notice board warned of forest fires and displayed park regulations. There were two picnic tables nearby plus the litter can. "You can start back to the car if you want."

"I'll come with you," Kelsey said, trying to atone for her behavior.

Brent didn't answer her, setting off across the deserted picnic area as if he couldn't wait to start back to Santa Fe. Kelsey chewed unhappily on her lower lip and followed him, wishing the set of those broad shoulders wasn't quite so daunting.

She was so intent on catching up that she didn't pay attention to where she was walking. Before she knew what was happening, she'd slipped on an uneven stone at the edge of the path. Her injured ankle gave way and she uttered a startled gasp as she plunged forward. Her hands went out to break her fall, allowing the vacuum bottle to drop and hit the ground with a sound of breaking glass.

She was dimly conscious of Brent's arrested figure in front of her. Then he came striding back to help even as she sat up and dusted the grit from her palms.

"Are you all right?" He dropped the lunch boxes and came down on one knee beside her. "Don't try to get up!"

"I'm certainly not going to stay here rolling around in the dirt for the rest of the afternoon." She grimaced as she discovered a sharp piece of gravel embedded in her thumb. "Dammit all!"

Brent misinterpreted her annoyance for pain and reached for her bandaged ankle. "I hope to God that you haven't made things worse. Hold still, you little idiot!" The last came as she attempted to pull her shoe from his grasp and gasped as she twisted her foot the wrong way.

After that, she gave up trying to explain, waiting until he'd rechecked the bandage and waggled her foot gently to test it. Finally he said, "I don't think you've done any more damage. Try putting some weight on it. Just lean on me while I lift you—there now! How's that?"

"It's okay." Kelsey pushed the hair back from her face with her dusty fingers as she met his concerned gaze. "That's what I was trying to tell you. I just slipped. Nothing was damaged except my pride—and the thermos." Bending over to retrieve the broken bottle, she added, "It might as well go with the rest of the garbage."

Brent collected it without comment but his glance narrowed as he saw her scratched hand. "That needs some attention. Wait here and I'll get some water from the stream to mop you up."

Kelsey started to protest, to tell him that she could certainly manage by herself. Then she remembered the steep bank next to their lunch spot and decided that the way things were going, she'd probably distinguish herself by falling down and trying to drown herself in the attempt.

She *did* manage to dispose of the lunch remains in the litter receptacle before Brent returned with a damp handkerchief. His eyebrows went up when he saw where she was, but all he said was, "Come on— let's do the repair work in the car. You might as well be comfortable."

She sighed and started down the path. "I don't know why you bother."

"Hey, what *is* this?" He caught her elbow and gently pulled her around to face him on the deserted path. His deliberate glance assessed her pale cheeks, the smudges beneath her blue eyes, and noted the effort it took to keep her lips from trembling.

Kelsey defiantly tried to outstare him but poise deserted her when she was just inches away from his tall figure. It was an effort for her not to reach up and touch that strand of thick dark hair that fell over his forehead, even as she watched. It gave him a younger look, strangely at variance with the brooding expression on his rugged features just then.

Her own glance must have unwittingly reflected the yearning she felt. She heard him draw in his breath sharply and his clasp tightened on her arm as he bent toward her, muttering something rough and indistinguishable in his throat.

Kelsey couldn't help herself; she responded as eagerly and naturally as a flower to the sun, arching her body when his grasp moved possessively down to her hips and parting her lips at the touch of his mouth. His kiss wasn't gentle even at the beginning but as the seconds passed, it probed and demanded still more—shattering any remnants of self-control.

There was no telling how long the embrace would have gone on or the eventual outcome, if it hadn't been abruptly terminated by a commotion from the parking lot. The school buses last seen at the fish hatchery down the road arrived with a squeal of brakes, matched only by the squeals of the passengers as they prepared to disgorge at the lunch stop.

Fortunately, the childish voices preceded their actual arrival, so by the time the buses stopped rolling, Brent had dropped his arms and stepped back. It took Kelsey an instant longer to recover. She swayed and looked up at him dazedly.

"Are you all right?" His voice was brusque again, almost unfriendly.

"Yes." She swallowed and tried again. "Yes, of course."

Was that *all* he was going to say, she wondered distractedly. It was like a tape recording—he'd been uttering those same four words ever since he'd picked her up off the roadway hours before. And while his concern was certainly commendable, it wasn't what she wanted to hear after those draining kisses and caresses that still had her trembling.

"Unless you want to go steady with the third grade, we should get out of here," Brent announced after another look around. "That would really put the final touches to the day."

Kelsey was so frozen with misery by then that she couldn't have answered, even if she'd anything to say.

She trailed him back to the parking lot, moving

aside on the path when a shrieking parcel of children bearing lunch sacks headed toward the picnic site they'd just deserted.

The front seat of the car didn't bring any immediate relief. Brent's rangy form barely managed to fit into the crowded quarters, so he simply handed over the dampened handkerchief, letting her clean the grit from her palms. There was a smudge on the linen, showing that he must have dropped it on the ground sometime during their embrace, but he didn't offer any explanations and Kelsey would have perished before she mentioned it.

When she had finished, she draped the damp cloth over the glove compartment and managed to say, "All set and ready to go again. I think I can manage to ride back to Santa Fe without falling out of the car or getting my feet tangled in the floor mat."

"So no more 'kiss it and make it well' therapy is necessary?" Brent had started the car and was edging it out onto the main road as he made the careless remark.

Kelsey's cheeks lost the last of their color. So *that's* all it was, she thought woodenly. Brent didn't need to carry a big stick; he could flatten his victims without moving a finger.

"Next time you might furnish a game plan," she managed in a cool tone. "Or at least warn a person what you have in mind. Maybe Geraldine appreciates those caveman tactics, but I'm used to a more subtle approach."

The car's speed surged as Brent leaned on the accelerator, although his expression didn't change.

"It's nice to know that you haven't been pining away all these months without having any fun."

Kelsey turned and pointedly watched the ponderosa pines go whizzing past on her side of the road before glancing at her watch. "At least we'll be getting back to the house in good time."

"We would be if that's where we were headed." He shot her a careless glance, adding, "I promised a friend who works at the Pecos Monument that I'd drop some papers off for him. It's not much out of our way and it'll save making another trip tomorrow. I didn't think you'd mind."

It was such a reasonable request that Kelsey couldn't very well object, especially since he knew very well that she didn't have any real plans for the day. The main reason she'd wanted to get back to the house was to avoid him for the rest of the afternoon and give her nerve endings a chance to uncurl.

"It doesn't matter one way or the other," she said. "Unless Daisy is pining."

"You saw Daisy when we left. Only a break in the chow line would upset her seriously." His voice was bland. "Have you ever been to the Monument?"

Kelsey shook her head and then, realizing that his attention was on the traffic ahead, said hastily, "No—but I've always wanted to see it."

"You should enjoy it. There's a trail through the ruins of the church and convent plus a restored *kiva*, if I remember."

"I should know what a *kiva* is but . . ."

"Your education *has* been neglected," Brent replied, obviously amused. "It's a ceremonial chamber. They're still in use today."

Kelsey could have told him that after what had happened at the picnic area, she was lucky to know how her name was spelled, let alone display any aptitude on Indian lore.

Brent continued, saying, "There's a *horno* oven in the visitor compound—you can try the bread some of the tribal women bake while I'm getting rid of those papers."

"There's no need for me to sit around. I'd like to explore some of the ruins."

"Look! Let's not argue about it—the whole point of this maneuver is to—" He broke off abruptly as if he'd said more than he'd intended.

"Is to what?"

A stubborn silence greeted her question and a quick look at his set jawline showed Kelsey that he wouldn't volunteer any more information.

Not that she needed much. It was becoming increasingly evident that he was keeping her out of circulation as a precautionary measure rather than any sentimental impulse to revisit old haunts.

Kelsey decided that being tagged a responsibility didn't do much for her ego and she stared unhappily at the passing landscape as the car increased speed.

The encroaching overcast was winning out over the good weather to the south and the remaining rays of sunshine were a pale attempt, doing little to soften harsh outlines of the valley they entered as the road wound out of the foothills. The high river valley's short growing season limited crop cultivation, which left grazing as the chief resource. That afternoon, the livestock was out of sight in the fenced acreage, only scattered outbuildings of the ranches remaining as evidence of civilization.

Brent must have noticed Kelsey's interest in the surroundings. "Do you know anything about this place where we're going?" he asked finally in a friendlier tone.

"Not a whole lot. Someone told me that the ruins of the church were a landmark for travelers on the Santa Fe Trail. There's not much else left to see, is there?"

He shook his head. "Disease and war with the Comanches put the final touches to the place. There were only seventeen people in the pueblo when they left in 1838."

Kelsey nodded as she surveyed the austere landscape which appeared almost monochromatic in the thin afternoon sunlight. "It couldn't have been an easy life for them around here."

"Yet they managed for almost four hundred years. The location helped—they were between the buffalo hunters of the plains and the farming tribes who lived in the Rio Grande. Legend has it that they did very well for themselves in the early days. When the Franciscan Fathers arrived, they introduced wheat and the beehive oven."

"And most of the livestock, too, didn't they?"

"You're absolutely right—go to the head of the class."

"Plus adobe building blocks that they used to construct their missions," Kelsey said, happy to be on a friendly wavelength again. "Norman told me all about it. He saw the 'eye of God' symbol that I hung in Lucius's kitchen and knew that I was interested in Indian lore," she added without thinking and then could have kicked herself as she saw the warmth in Brent's expression cool immediately.

"Very commendable. There's a good pottery exhibition at the visitor center. You'll have to ask Norman to bring you back for your next visit," Brent said, effectively putting an end to the discussion.

Kelsey muttered something about "she'd do that" and sank back onto the seat. If she couldn't utter more than a sentence without causing another skirmish, it was better if she'd just pretend to be enthralled with the scenery. The old days when she and Brent spent hours exchanging hopes and dreams were apparently gone forever.

The gray overcast had triumphed completely by the time he turned into the gravel road leading to the Pecos National Monument and a brisk breeze was bending the grasses alongside the car. Kelsey saw the one-story buildings of the visitor center through a haze as a strong gust of wind sent dust from an adjoining field in front of the car, momentarily obliterating the outlines of the restored church walls and a *kiva* on the south pueblo. Then the air cleared, and the neat adobe block walls which transversed the monument reappeared as Brent drove into the spacious parking lot.

"Looks as if the weather has discouraged most of the visitors," he commented, noting only a van over by the Indian oven and an official government car pulled up in front of the visitors' center. "It may be a little breezy for you."

"I'm not apt to be blown away," Kelsey assured him. "I'd like to watch that woman weaving baskets over by the oven—they do some wonderful things with bear grass and chokeberry branches here in the Southwest. If you don't mind," she added diffidently.

"It sounds fine," he said quickly, as if relieved that she didn't ask to accompany him. "You should be able to shelter from the wind behind the wall over there, and if they're baking bread, there'll be coffee to go along with it. I should be finished in"—he broke off to glance at his watch—"fifteen minutes at the most. You can come back to the car if you get tired earlier. Is that all right with you?" The last query came after he braked and turned off the ignition.

"Fine." Kelsey tried to sound as if she meant it. She noticed that he didn't bother to retrieve papers or anything else from the trunk before he disappeared into the visitors' center and closed the door behind him. Which meant that he either had the material for his purported visit in his shirt pocket or that he simply manufactured an excuse to visit the Monument. Kelsey frowned as she gazed around the almost-deserted grounds again. The place might be a treasure trove of history but it was hardly a valid reason for Brent to detour miles out of the way.

She was still looking thoughtful as she got out of the car herself. The first gust of wind made her fasten her jacket around her and be thankful that she'd brought it along.

The changeable weather evidently didn't bother the middle-aged Indian weaver because she was wearing just a cotton blouse and a long skirt of the same material as she sat on a mat, her fingers sorting deftly through the grasses piled at her side. A moment later, she was working a strand of bear grass into the half-finished basket in front of her.

"You like basketwork?" she asked when Kelsey smiled and lingered in obvious admiration.

"Very much. That's a pretty combination of colors. Do you sell the pieces when you're finished?"

The woman nodded. "I can't keep up with the orders. Most days when I'm here, there are tourists all over the place. They come to buy bread over there"—she jerked her head toward the deserted bakery counter—"but the weather must have discouraged everybody this afternoon. I'm ready to go home, too." Her expression sharpened at the sound of an engine starting nearby. She surged to her feet and stared out at the parked van which Kelsey had noticed when they arrived. "What's he think he's doing?" the woman muttered angrily.

"I'd say he's getting ready to leave," Kelsey said, her attention on the figure hunched behind the steering wheel.

"Not without me," the basket weaver announced. She swept the half-finished basket and her supply of reeds against the wall behind her and snatched up a worn purse. "He promised to take me into town today."

By then, the driver of the van had backed and was turning toward the exit from the parking lot. He had to slam on his brakes as the basket lady shouted and ran toward him, waving a frantic hand.

A minute later, she'd opened the door on the passenger side and climbed aboard. The van started up again and when it passed the bakery and oven Kelsey could see the weaver gesturing angrily as she told off the driver.

"So much for the lesson in basketry," Kelsey murmured wryly to herself. She walked over to the base of the wall and knelt to investigate the intricate pattern on the basket and then got to her feet again.

Shoving her hands in her jeans pockets to keep warm, she strolled over to inspect the deserted bakery counter where a few crumbs on a foil pan were all that remained of the morning's offerings. Even the fire in the *horno* oven nearby was dying down to embers. She stood in front of its welcome warmth for a minute or so, wondering what to do next.

The prospect of going back to sit in the car wasn't enthralling and she hesitated to interrupt Brent and his friend in the visitors' center. It *was* a temptation—if for no other reason than to annoy Brent. Kelsey thought about it and finally decided that she'd done enough childish things for the day. She'd go back to the car and search for something to read in the glove compartment while she waited.

It was the stray piece of paper blowing along a path nearby which diverted her attention to that part of the grounds. She strolled across to read the notice board posted beside it and found a diagram of the Ruins Trails which apparently wound throughout the most important excavations and restorations. They were all neatly numbered and seemed far more interesting than waiting in a cold car.

At least that was what she intended to tell Brent if he complained later. Probably she could see one or two of the attractions on the trail and be back before he even knew that she'd gone. Especially since he thought she was still standing around the Indian display center.

It was almost eerily quiet as she started down the path of hard-packed earth. Only her footsteps in the fine gravel which had been sifted on the surface broke the afternoon's silence. At the first curve of the trail she saw a neat pile of buckets and ladders, showing that workmen had been on the scene earlier. Maybe the darkening sky had discouraged them, too, Kelsey thought as she shivered involuntarily in the breeze. She looked over her shoulder and then shook her head ruefully. Heaven knew what she expected to see! Probably some of those spirits from the past mentioned on the historical legend at the beginning of the trail.

At least they'd be friendly spirits, Kelsey decided as she arrived at the first restoration. And they couldn't help but be pleased with the work which had been done to the large communal building, faithfully following the original architecture of the *convento*. She walked on after reading about the store rooms and weaving rooms around the patio. Just beyond were the tannery and livestock corral—all necessary to the early mission life.

By then, Kelsey's ankle was throbbing again but she made her way across to the restored *kiva* in the convent courtyard, peering down into the underground ceremonial room. There was a sign nearby telling about the faithful restoration of the Indian worshiping place, but after reading it, Kelsey still felt irresistibly drawn to the peeled wooden ladder which descended into the *kiva*.

It looked almost black down below and the rungs

of the ladder were exactly what the doctor at the clinic had told her to avoid. On the other hand, she argued to herself, there'd never be a better chance to see an Indian *kiva*.

She glanced over her shoulder again at the deserted courtyard where the shadows from the walls of the restored buildings were growing longer and more murky by the second. Then her gaze went upward to judge how long she had before the gathering gray clouds opened for a late-afternoon downpour.

"Not long," she murmured uneasily. "I'd better get a move on." Either that or be forced to use the ceiling of the *kiva* as an impromptu umbrella.

She went carefully down the rungs of the ladder, trying to avoid twisting her ankle whenever possible. Once she reached the hard-packed earth floor of the subterranean ceremonial chamber, she gave a sigh of relief and stood quietly for a moment, letting her eyes adjust to the gloom.

The shadows engulfing the room hid the imperfections of the chamber's walls. They also charitably blurred the beams on the ceiling which probably housed a good-sized insect population. Kelsey prudently kept her hands in her jacket pockets as she explored the room with its altarlike prominence made of adobe and the firepit with its blackened center. She shivered suddenly, aware that the chilled air had a damp earthy smell—almost as if she'd wandered into a burial chamber.

Which was utter nonsense, she told herself, and then cocked her head as she heard the sound of a male voice. It had to come from the visitors' center, she rationalized, and her pulse accelerated as she realized it was probably Brent trying to find her.

"Damn!" she murmured then, guiltily aware that she'd spent far longer in her exploration than she'd intended. She retraced her footsteps across the *kiva* and started up the ladder, intent on trying to get back to the parking lot before Brent discovered how far she'd gone afield.

She was on the middle of the ladder, her head just emerging into the daylight when her eyes lit on a pair of trouser-clad legs standing by the *kiva* entrance. Her gaze shot upward, and she almost lost her hold on the wood when she heard the whiplash of Brent's greeting.

"Get the hell out of there before I do something we'll both regret!"

Kelsey was so surprised by his vehemence that she couldn't have taken another step if she'd tried to.

Brent's eyes narrowed at her reaction. "Maybe you didn't hear me," he said in a soft monotone that made Kelsey's knuckles go white on the ladder.

He leaned toward her and it was all she could do not to scuttle back down to the *kiva*—anywhere—away from his anger. "I heard you," she managed to say finally. "I don't know what your trouble is, but I'd appreciate it if you'd move out of the way. I want to get off this thing."

"And I'd like to know why in the devil you're on it." He made no attempt to help her, neither did he change his position.

Kelsey hesitated an instant longer. Then she tightened her grip on the ladder and went on up. As she stepped out of the hole, she chose the side away from Brent and tried to swallow a gasp as her tender ankle gave way on the sloping dirt.

Only then did Brent's hand shoot out, catching her elbow to pull her toward the parking lot as if he had her on a leash.

"You don't have to treat me like Daisy," Kelsey complained, trying unsuccessfully to keep up with his long strides.

"The dog would have more sense," he tossed over his shoulder.

"That's because I didn't go to obedience school. And I don't intend to," she snarled back. "*Would* you let go of my elbow or do you plan to drag me all the way to the car?"

He stopped short, causing Kelsey to almost run into him. "Don't tempt me," he said through clenched teeth. "Or so help me, I'll turn you over my knee right here and now. After that, you'll have a hell of a lot more trouble sitting down than walking."

"You wouldn't dare!"

"Don't be more of a damned fool than you have to. I've spent the entire day riding herd on you to try and keep you out of trouble. All you had to do was sit over there and drink coffee . . ."

"There wasn't any . . ."

"Then you could have waited in the car." His icy stare looked like Lake Michigan in midwinter. "You remember the car? That thing down there with locks on the doors?"

"You don't have to be sarcastic!"

"And you didn't have to decide to tour the whole bloody Monument on your own. You stood out like a

135

sore thumb on the landscape and then decided to make it even easier by disappearing into a hole in the ground. The only thing you missed was spraining the other ankle on that damned ladder."

"I could have fallen down on my head," she said, trying to match his insouciance.

"That happened earlier on. Why didn't you warn me that I was dealing with a pinhead?" He started walking again, leaving her to trail uncertainly behind.

"Brent, I'm sorry . . ." The knowledge that she was in the wrong showed in the tone of her voice. "I didn't mean to worry anybody. It wasn't deliberate."

"Famous last words." He shrugged as he turned to look at her. "At least, you got away with it this time."

She frowned and hurried to catch up with him. "I don't understand. What did you think would happen?" Her voice sharpened. "You might have the decency to clue me in on all this."

His face was tired and he sounded as if he'd almost reached the end of his tether as they drew up beside the car. "If I could—I would. You'll have to trust me, Kelsey. A little longer, at least."

"I do, Brent." Kelsey's hand went out to his arm in an impulsive gesture. "Honestly. Besides," she said, trying to make a joke of it, "you scared the life out of me when I came up from that *kiva*. For a minute, I wasn't sure whose side you were on . . ." As her words trailed off she looked up at him for reassurance.

It didn't come. There wasn't anything in his expression to comfort her as he reached down and removed her hand from his sleeve. While it involved part of unlocking the car door, she knew very well that his gesture had been a deliberate one as well, erecting an invisible but very real barrier between them. His slow comment added strength to it. "If I were you, Kelsey, I wouldn't take chances on anybody from here on. You simply can't afford to."

Chapter 7

KELSEY slid into the front seat without any more conversation. Reaction really set in when Brent started the car and turned back toward the highway. Kelsey felt tears well up behind her eyelids and she shifted to stare out the window beside her so he wouldn't know how much his second snub of the afternoon had affected her.

Even though she was careful not to make the slightest noise, Brent must have had an inkling of her thoughts because he broke the silence before they'd gone a half-mile on the road to Santa Fe.

"We have reason to believe that one of the employees back at the Monument was involved in your brake 'accident' this morning," he began slowly. "I didn't tell you before because I didn't want to worry you."

Kelsey was so startled that she turned to face him, forgetting the telltale streaks on her cheeks which she'd been determined to hide. "I don't understand. Why, I don't know anybody who even works there!" Her damp lashes widened as another thought occurred to her. "Unless it was somebody with a grudge against you. Is that it?"

"In a way." Brent took his time, searching for the right words. "To be honest, I've never met him. The last thing I suspected was that he'd be on tap while we were there."

"You mean that you were actually talking to him in the visitor center?" There was incredulity in Kelsey's voice as she tried to imagine it.

"Lord, no!" Brent shot her an impatient look. "You make it sound like some kind of a shootout at the corral. I just went there to talk to the man in charge. It wasn't until afterward that we discovered our 'brake mechanic' was on the grounds." When a puzzled silence greeted his words, Brent said tersely, "Not until we saw the van going out to the highway. For a God-awful minute, I thought you might be in it with him."

"You mean the truck that picked up the weaving lady?" At his nod, Kelsey frowned and then announced, "You're crazy. There wasn't anything sinister about that. The driver was just giving her a ride back to town."

"I didn't say there was anything wrong about that." Brent sounded as if he were hanging on to his patience with an effort. "It's standard operating procedure at the native center. Except that today it was supposed to be the regular man who gave it to her. Our friend took his place—apparently he decided not to hang around after he saw us drive in."

"Oh." Kelsey had to swallow as she considered the implications. "I still don't see why you were so mad at me," she continued after a minute. "I didn't get near the van. From the way you acted at the *kiva*, anybody would have thought that I'd been on the curb thumbing a ride."

"I just told you. For a while, we didn't know where the hell you were. Not until I saw you bobbing around out there on the landscape where you weren't supposed to be. And then it occurred to me—if not to you—that maybe the creep had a friend. In which case, you were making it damned easy for them, heading for a funeral chamber without an invitation."

Kelsey's shoulders sagged as his voice lashed her. "I said I was sorry. Even so, you could have warned me ahead of time."

"I was hoping that you wouldn't have to know—until it was all over."

"Well, isn't it? All over, I mean? Now that you know who it was, the police just have to pick him up." Her bright tone wavered as she saw him slowly shake his head. "Except that there's more, isn't there?"

Brent's tone was wry as he confirmed it. "You've got it in one. And that's the reason why I don't want you doing any more damned-fool shenanigans until this thing's wrapped up."

"But if it's *you* they're after . . ."

"We don't know that for sure. Apparently you've been pulled in on the fringes of this mess. And as your friendly neighborhood banker would say— there's a substantial penalty for early withdrawal." Brent slowed as the car came up behind a hay truck and then he accelerated to go around the slower-moving vehicle. When they were safely past, he said, "That's why you're not to do anything different from usual—except that you do it under supervision."

Kelsey was more shaken by Brent's words than she chose to admit but she kept her tone light. "Don't tell me that Daisy's actually a guard dog in disguise?"

"From what I've seen, that dog would welcome Attila the Hun if he came calling with a sirloin steak."

There wasn't any more conversation after that. The traffic thickened when they neared the suburbs of Santa Fe and Kelsey tried to improve her mood by concentrating on the beauty of the city's residential districts. Even the first sprinkling of rain couldn't dim the colorful gardens or the charm of adobe walls which allowed just fleeting glimpses of household patios. Beyond the city, the Sangre de Cristo and Jemez Mountains took on the gray of the overcast sky, making Kelsey marvel again at the many faces of the New Mexico high country. It was hard to believe how bright and cheerful the sun had been at the beginning of the day. Considering all that had happened, it had been a false portent in more ways than one.

Brent made a left turn off the highway just then, bringing her attention back to the present. "This isn't the way home," she pointed out.

He waited until he'd turned onto another angled street before agreeing with her. "I know, but Vera isn't in any hurry to leave. I phoned when I was back at the Monument and told her we might have dinner downtown. Is Mexican food all right with you?"

"I—I guess so. But I'm not really dressed to go

anyplace." She gestured down at her jeans. "Rolling around in the dirt doesn't help."

"You look fine to me," Brent said easily. "If you're really worried, you can do some running repairs at the restaurant. We're a few minutes early for our reservation."

"You *have* been busy. Have you decided what we're going to eat, too?"

Brent slowed beside a sprawling building which was once part of Santa Fe's historic Guadalupe Mission complex. "If I remember, you always ordered *burritos* with a side order of *sopapillas*," he said blandly. "Or have you gone on to different things these days?"

Kelsey waited until he'd parked and turned off the ignition before she had nerve to say, "You could at least have asked if I wanted to eat here."

Brent appeared to consider it. Finally he nodded as he got out of the car and came around to open her door. "You're right. I could have."

Kelsey was loath to let the subject die a well-deserved death. "You mean—that's all there is to it as far as you're concerned. My opinion doesn't matter."

"If picking a restaurant is so important to you— you can do it nonstop for the rest of the year as far as I'm concerned. In the meantime, stop sulking!" He put his hand in the middle of her back none-too-gently after that pronouncement, to escort her to the restaurant's front door. The only way Kelsey could have objected further would have been to stage a sit-in on the steps or some other equally nonsensical maneuver, so she decided to yield—having made her point.

When Brent escorted her into the crowded foyer, he muttered in a low voice, "I realize that you're feeling under the weather, but don't fight me, Kelsey. Not tonight, at least. Another time I can give you my full attention." His hand moved from her back to catch her fingers in a warm clasp. "Why don't you go in and brush off some of that dust. I'll order us a drink in the bar . . ." He broke off to grin down at her. "Better tell me what you'd like before you disappear."

"But you know that I always have a Margarita when we eat Mexican food," Kelsey replied automatically before she realized that she'd fallen neatly into the trap. She smiled at him. "I guess I deserved that. I promise to forgive you if you'll order some *nachos* to go with it."

"I always do." His grin broadened before he walked into the room on the right where people occupied most of the tables as well as sitting along an old-fashioned bar on one wall.

Kelsey threaded her way through the parties waiting to be shown into the dining room which occupied the newer *sala* in another wing. She was glad to discover that the ladies room was empty so she was able to brush the rest of the dust from her jeans without being subject to curious stares. Hot water plus judicious use of powder and lipstick helped in the transformation. By the time she'd brushed her hair and smoothed on a faintest application of eye makeup, she decided that she wouldn't disgrace Brent when she walked into the dining room with him. A leather jacket and jeans certainly weren't what she would have chosen to wear out to dinner but fortunately Santa Fe residents were informal in their dress. And since the restaurant boasted wonderful food, attention would be centered on the menu.

She walked back to the foyer, exchanging a greeting with the frankly admiring maitre d' on the way. By the time she reached the entrance to the bar, she'd decided that she'd have to apologize to Brent once again. If he *had* consulted her, she probably would have chosen the very same place.

There was a smile on her lips as she paused expectantly in the doorway and glanced around the crowded barroom, trying to locate him. Her gaze skimmed the tables as she waited for a beckoning hand or a hail.

When nothing of the kind occurred, a slight frown creased her forehead. Surely he wouldn't have gone on into the dining room without leaving word.

She started toward the end of the bar to ask the nearest waiter if a message had been left for her. She was maneuvering through a foursome of guests leaving to keep their dinner reservation when she stopped so suddenly that one of the men almost fell over her.

"I'm sorry, miss. I didn't hurt you, did I?" he asked as he regained his balance.

"No, I'm fine. Besides, it was my fault," Kelsey assured him as she sidestepped to the end of the bar where the waiters congregated to fill their table orders. Kelsey tried to stay out of their way, keeping behind the cash register where they rang up their checks as her gaze riveted on the end of the room again.

Brent's figure stood out commandingly from the

other customers at the far end of the bar, but it was his companion who attracted the bulk of attention—especially from the other men in the vicinity. Geraldine's brunette beauty had never looked more striking than in the red lace cocktail dress she was wearing. There was a short jacket which nipped in at the waist for a decorous touch but it did nothing to hide the halter neckline of the dress which was cut daringly low. A critical observer might have said that Geraldine looked stuffed into it but a more accurate description would have been overstuffed. It was that excess which had every man within twenty feet waiting for her to make a sudden move.

From what Kelsey could see, Brent was no exception. He may have been concentrating on Geraldine's lovely upturned face but he didn't retreat when she deliberately raised her arms and put them around his neck. Despite the crowd of people, Kelsey saw Brent bend his head toward the inviting lips she offered.

Kelsey couldn't watch any longer. She turned blindly toward the restaurant foyer, barely avoiding a catastrophe with a waitress carrying a trayful of drinks on the way.

The restaurant hostess saw Kelsey's pallor when she hesitated by the reservation desk at the entrance. "Is there anything I can get for you?"

Kelsey wanted to say there certainly was. Preferably a bucket of boiling oil with a tray of feathers on the side to pour over the two poisonous snakes still standing by the bar. Instead she drew a deep shuddering breath and had to be content with, "It's nothing. I just need a little fresh air. It was stuffy in the other room with so many people. If I could stand here for a moment . . ."

"Of course." The receptionist sounded relieved that she didn't have a crisis on her hands as well as too many people on the reservation list for dinner. "You're not a bit in the way. I'll come back and check on how you're feeling as soon as I get this party of twelve seated."

"Thanks—you're very kind." Kelsey leaned against the wall to be out of the stream of incoming dinner guests and pushed her hair back from her face as she tried to think. One sure thing—she wouldn't go back in the bar. And as for Brent, no wonder that miserable fiend had made the restaurant reservation beforehand. He hadn't the nerve to mention that dinner had been for three all along!

The ring-tailed, two-timing louse! Kelsey saw the cashier casting an anxious glance toward her, and decided it would be better if she went outside at that point—otherwise, the management might send for the men in white coats. Or, even worse, Brent and Geraldine might come looking for her.

There wasn't a secluded spot near the restaurant entrance so Kelsey automatically started toward the parking lot. Her steps faltered and then stopped entirely as she realized she had a set of car keys in her purse. What an idiot she was! Wandering around the landscape like some displaced person when she owned a perfectly good automobile just around the corner.

She started walking again, this time with purposeful steps toward the object in question. Brent would be incensed, she told herself as she pulled up beside the car and unlocked the door. As she slid in the driver's seat and turned on the ignition, she decided he'd never forgive her for making him look foolish in front of Geraldine. If luck was really in, Geraldine might be depending on him for a ride home. That would really make the egg hit the fan!

Kelsey's face wore a grim smile as she drove through the edge of the business district to get on the arterial heading north. For all its many cosmopolitan features, Santa Fe was the devil itself when it came to public transportation. There was a regular airport bus for Albuquerque but the town's only taxicab company had gone out of business earlier in the year.

Not that Kelsey had hopes of discommoding Brent for long. But if she could even dent that monumental self-assurance of his, it would be her only hope of salvation.

No, not the only hope, she told herself as her foot pressed down on the accelerator and the car sped homeward through the twilight dusk. There was one other way to save herself further heartbreak. She'd been a coward once before when it came to dealing with Brent and, even though she wasn't proud of her behavior then, there was nothing wrong with putting a considerable distance between them this time. A woman would be a fool to stay around and let him shred her emotions at will. Geraldine could have the field to herself. She'd already won the battle, if that scene at the bar was to be believed.

Vera's gray head poked around the front door a little later when Kelsey's car pulled up in the driveway. "Wouldn't you know!" she said. "I just hung

147

up the phone before I saw you turn off the road. Brent wondered if you'd arrived home." She smiled as Kelsey came up on the porch and opened the door a careful slit further. "Just a minute till I get hold of Daisy's collar—she's hard to lasso if she gets outside. There! Now it's safe."

Kelsey quickly edged through the door and managed to shut it behind her before the Airedale pulled free. An instant later, she was rocked backward by two forceful paws on her shoulders, and a cold, wet nose pressed against her cheek. "Daisy—get down!" she scolded, but she hugged the rough head before pushing the dog back to the floor. "I hope you've behaved yourself some of the time, at least." She looked at Vera who was smiling broadly. "Good news or bad? Are the legs still on the bed and the upholstery on the davenport?"

"The furniture's fine." Vera bit her lip and then confessed. "I hope you won't be too upset about losing the inner sole of your navy blue pumps. Daisy got in the closet when I wasn't looking."

Kelsey made a relieved gesture. "If that's the extent of the damage . . ."

"Well, she did find that big foil-wrapped peppermint that you'd left on the bureau."

"Daisy—you beast!" Kelsey tried to direct a quelling glance at the dog nuzzling her side but Daisy chose to ignore it. "It isn't serious," Kelsey confided to Vera. "I didn't need the extra calories."

"Neither did she. That dog's spent most of the day watching the refrigerator."

"First things first." Kelsey grinned at the Airedale. "You'll look like a barrel if you keep that up."

"Exactly what I told her," Vera said, "and I know what I'm talking about. But that's enough of that. You'd better phone Brent. He sounded real het-up when he called. Just like your friend Mr. Wilkens."

"Norman? You mean he called, too?"

"Why, yes. I told Brent when he phoned me earlier from the Monument." Vera's expression was troubled as she saw Kelsey frown. "Did he forget to let you know?"

"It must have slipped his mind."

"Oh, dear. And Mr. Wilkens wanted his proofs back. I think he said the deadline was tomorrow. Or was it today?"

"You mean he brought them here . . ." Kelsey broke off to shove Daisy's derriere off her injured foot. "You weigh a ton. Why don't you go sit someplace else—that's a girl. No, I'm not going to take you for a walk."

"She keeps dragging that leash around, too," Vera said beaming like a proud parent.

"It's blackmail. Maybe later, you demanding dog." Kelsey put the leash back on the hall table before turning to Vera. "Where are the things that Norman left?"

"Right in on the kitchen counter. I put them there so they'd be out of reach of 'you-know-who.'" Vera bustled into the kitchen followed by the other two and handed a manila envelope to Kelsey. "He was real upset this forenoon when he found that you were gone for the day."

"I should have called him. Well, I can do it now." Kelsey reached for the phone at the end of the kitchen counter. "Did he leave word where he'd be?"

"Part of the time at the Opera House, I think. He muttered something about damned rehearsals and damned dogs as he went out."

"Damned dogs?" That was too much for Kelsey. "You mean Daisy? Why was he mad at her?"

"Well, she'd been rooting around trying to unwrap that peppermint just before he came to the door and she had some chocolate on her whiskers."

Kelsey closed her eyes for a minute to gather her strength and then opened them again. "I can see it now. She managed to wipe her whiskers on his trousers."

"Tan trousers. I did my best to get the stain off the knees, but chocolate . . ." Vera shook her head.

"I'd better phone right now."

Vera watched her start to dial. "I left the number where Brent can be reached on that pad by the cookie jar. If you don't need me anymore, I'll go get my things together."

Kelsey nodded and helped herself to a cookie while the phone rang at Norman's number. She let it ring for a full thirty seconds before hanging up. "Damn," she muttered as she thumbed through the revised advertising proofs for the program and noted the printer's deadline at the top. Why couldn't Norman have taken them with him instead of insisting that she check them, too? Absently she helped herself to another cookie, and when a throaty whine came from the dog sitting in front of her, she said, "No deal, scrounge. You've probably been eating these all day. Isn't that right, Vera?"

The older woman had just reentered the kitchen, her coat in her arms. "Lordy, yes. That dog doesn't need any more nourishment for a week. Did you reach Brent yet?"

"I didn't try," Kelsey said, loath to furnish an explanation. "It looks as if I'll have to go out again and track down Mr. Wilkens to return these proofs. I'm not having any luck at his apartment."

Vera's normally cheerful face took on a troubled cast. "It's pretty late in the day for that, isn't it? What with your ankle and all."

"Oh, that's much better," Kelsey assured her blithely, if not quite truthfully. "And you go right ahead with your own plans. I'll take Daisy in the car with me."

"It'll be dark before long."

Kelsey was well aware of the drawbacks to her scheme and wasn't looking forward to an extra trip back to town. On the other hand, she suspected that Brent might have warned Vera to prevent just such a jaunt until he could get there personally.

"With any luck, I can run Norman down at the Opera House first thing," she told the older woman. "I might even get a dinner out of it."

"I thought you were going to eat with Brent."

"Something came up to change our plans. It doesn't matter, I'm not very hungry."

Vera came over to pointedly move the cookie jar out of reach. "You should be— after all that's happened. I'd better stay and fix you a decent dinner."

Kelsey put an impulsive arm around the other's plump shoulders. "No way. There's no telling how

151

long it will take me to find Norman. You go on home."

"At least let me fix a cup of tea while you're changing," Vera urged. "You'll feel better afterward. Those jeans look as if they'd gone through a war."

And so they had, Kelsey thought. It was an effort to keep her voice cheerful. "I'd forgotten all about them. It's a good thing you mentioned it; Norman likes to see women neat and tidy."

"I didn't say it for that reason," Vera retorted. "You look plain tuckered-out. Are you sure that you can't wait for Brent to come home and take care of this for you?"

"Very sure. I *will* have a cup of tea with you after I change, though. Maybe I'll even get through to Norman when I phone again. I'll call from the bedroom."

Vera opened her mouth to protest and then obviously thought better of it. "You do that. I'll make some cinnamon toast to go with that tea."

Daisy was obviously torn between devotion to Kelsey and a ringside seat by the toaster. Calories won out but she performed escort duty down the hallway before returning to the kitchen.

Kelsey didn't linger over her change of clothes. She put on a long-sleeved shirt in a black-and-ivory print and then donned an ivory wrap skirt with a linen weave. Afterward she draped a black tailored jacket over her shoulders before surveying her shoe rack. There wasn't anything she could do to hide the bandage on her ankle but she tried on a pair of low-heeled pumps and decided they'd have to do.

She picked up the telephone to call Norman again

and had barely gotten it to her ear when Vera lifted the kitchen extension. The older woman immediately realized her mistake, saying, "I'm sorry, Kelsey. I'll make my call later—it isn't important." She put down the receiver and Kelsey waited an instant before dialing Norman's number. This time there was a busy signal, so she hung up and brushed her hair before trying again.

The phone barely finished the first ring before he answered, saying brusquely, "You're late! For God's sake, what are you trying to do to me, Gerry?"

"Gerry!" Kelsey gasped, completely thrown by his identification.

There was a sudden silence over the wire. Then Norman asked irritably, "Who *is* this? I'm in no mood to play games."

"Well, don't snap my head off. It's Kelsey, and obviously I've phoned at the wrong time. Do you want to call me back?"

"Kelsey, love—I'm sorry. I had no idea you were still on the face of the earth! Where in the devil have you been all day?"

"Well, Brent took me for a drive this morning—"

"Never mind. I can skip the scenario," Norman cut in. "How in hell am I going to get those proofs back on time?"

"I can drop them off at your place, if it's vital. Are you going to be there for a little while?"

There was another pause. Then he said carefully, "It depends. Actually, I'd made other plans, but my schedule's been thrown off."

Not only your schedule, but your love life as well, Kelsey decided. Especially if that first outburst of his meant what she thought. She wondered what his reaction would be if she told him where the beauteous Gerry was at that moment.

"Kelsey, are you still there?"

"Yes, but not for long. I have other things to do, too. Why don't I drop these proofs on your doorstep?"

"Because they're too important to leave untended."

"Well, there's always the Opera House. Can I leave the envelope there? You could pick it up tomorrow."

"I guess the gates are open tonight," he conceded. "There's a rehearsal of sorts. One of the baritones for the benefit wants to change arias—even this late in the scheme of things. Wouldn't you think he'd know better!"

"That sounds more like a prima donna than a baritone," Kelsey acknowledged. "How would it be if I left your proofs with him?"

"Use your head, Kelsey." Norman paused and then went on. "Oh, hell! I might as well meet you there. I can get together with—" He broke off, realizing he was on sticky ground.

"If you mean Geraldine, say so," Kelsey told him. "I'm surprised that you've been so quiet about her, that's all. Otherwise, it's none of my affair."

"Of course it is. You're my first love," he said lightly. "But we misjudged her part with Russ all along. Brent misquoted her in the interview. She told me so."

"Well, the three of you can resolve it without my help. I'm going back home tomorrow." A sound from the hallway made her turn to the doorway, half expecting Daisy to come bounding in the room.

The door stayed closed, however, and she forgot about the interruption when Norman's voice reverberated in the receiver. "I *knew* that it was a mistake for you to stay in that house with Brent. Tell him for me that—"

"He isn't here," she cut in tiredly. "And not apt to be for some time."

"What do you mean by that?"

"Exactly what it sounds like. I left him downtown. He had a dinner date."

Intuition must have told Norman that she was leaving out the important part of the story. "Not so fast," he said. "Let's have the rest of it."

"That's all there is," she said, deciding it was time for a white lie. "But if you want these proofs, I'll have to deliver them right away. There's a lot for me to do later tonight."

"Such as?"

"Packing. I *told* you . . ."

"Oh, that." He sounded scornful. "Brent'll talk you around, the way he always does. Don't think he's going to let you off the string."

"He already has." Kelsey had no desire to continue the conversation and it showed in her tone. "As far as I'm concerned, he can take a long walk on a short pier, and if you keep on giving me advice—you can join him."

"There's no need to get upset."

"Look, Norman, I'm tired and I'm hungry. Do I leave these proofs with the baritone or on your front porch?"

"I'll meet you at the Opera House."

"In the parking lot there?"

"Well, I'm not going to wait around outside in the rain," he told her aloofly. "Come on backstage. That way, I can do some work while I'm waiting for you."

Kelsey heard his receiver go down and waited an instant before lowering her own. From his tone, he was feeling far from happy. And he'd be a lot more unhappy if he knew where Geraldine was at that moment. Well, it served him right for playing around with the brunette, Kelsey decided uncharitably as she went out in the hall and walked to the kitchen.

"What's the matter? Bad news?" Vera asked, looking up from buttering some toast.

"Not really. I shouldn't stay to eat any of this," Kelsey said, picking up a piece from the top of the stack and shaking cinnamon sugar on it. "Mmmm—it tastes marvelous! I can see why Daisy sticks close."

"I've poured your tea," Vera said, sensibly ignoring Kelsey's opening statement as she pushed a bar stool over for her to sit on. "Are you sure that you can't take time for some real food?"

"This will be just fine. I'll heat some soup when I get back if I want anything more."

"I thought you were going out with Mr. Wilkens," Vera persisted, her voice showing that she wasn't crazy about that, either.

"Just long enough to return his proofs. He's going to meet me at the Opera House."

"Is it open at this time of night?"

"Norman says so. Something about an extra rehearsal." Kelsey scooped up a bit of melted butter before it could drop from a small piece of toast crust and then capitulated to Daisy's yearning muzzle. "That's absolutely the last morsel for you tonight. Well, I'd better get going." She swallowed the rest of her tea and picked up the manila envelope of proofs to take with her. Keeping a restraining hand on Daisy's collar, she decided to make sure of Vera's future work plans before finalizing her own. "You *will* be able to come every day from now on, won't you?"

"Why, yes. If you're sure you want me." The older woman looked at her quizzically.

"You're as welcome as the flowers of May," Kelsey said, not trying to hide her relief. At least Daisy wouldn't be left without a sitter, even if it wasn't the one Brent thought he'd hired.

"Don't forget to have something more to eat when you get back," Vera fussed. "A snack doesn't really count as dinner."

Kelsey was intent on fastening Daisy's leash in the front hall. It was not an easy task since the big dog was plunging around as if she were on a pogo stick. "There! Let me open the door—you don't have to claw it down." Kelsey caught sight of Vera, observing them from the kitchen archway. "I'd better take some more vitamins. Either that or hide Daisy's. Aren't you leaving now, too?"

"Not for a little while," Vera said, sounding slightly flustered. "I just remembered that the cat's still in the house. The last time I saw him he was sleeping out in the utility room."

"Elmo? He won't hurt anything. I can let him out when I come back."

"No, you go ahead. I want to slick up this kitchen, too."

"Well, for heaven's sake don't stick around to wash those tea things. I'll do them later." Kelsey couldn't linger any longer without losing an arm in the process as the big Airedale scrabbled to get off the porch.

The rain shower had tapered off momentarily, so Kelsey allowed her a quick walk around the driveway before opening the car door. She didn't unsnap the leash until she'd gotten in the car herself. "Now sit there and behave yourself until we get to the Opera House," she told the dog. "Then you can guard the car in the parking lot. And stop washing my ear or I'll have to comb my hair again when I get there."

Despite Daisy's enthusiasm, Kelsey found that it helped to have company as she drove back down the dirt road toward the highway. It was hard to dwell on her unhappy lot when the seventy-five-pound Airedale was sitting beside her, vibrating with *joie de vivre*. For all her failings, Daisy was a dear!

Kelsey braked before turning onto the freeway and took the opportunity to scratch the dog's ears. "You're too big to kidnap, sweetie, but I'll ask Vera to keep an eye on you. And if Geraldine tries anything, just lean on her—hard."

There wasn't time for any more advice after that because the early evening traffic headed toward Taos was thick and Kelsey had to concentrate on her driving. Fortunately, it wasn't long before the distinctive outlines of Santa Fe's outdoor theater could be seen ahead on a hillside to the left of the four-lane freeway.

Since there wasn't an opera scheduled, Kelsey was able to turn off the highway without trouble and make her way on the deserted two-lane road that wound up the hillside.

The earlier afternoon downpour had left the shrubbery borders dripping wet and they glistened when the car's headlights passed by. Outdoor spotlights scattered throughout the landscaping emphasized the extent of the acreage, but they also added to the desolation of the scene, making the trees cast eerie shadows along the hillside. The big Opera House itself looked like something from science fiction with its angular lines and a sweeping roof divided in two pieces. Contemporary design had won out in its construction, with a covered shell over the stage itself and another beamed roof over the rear part of the Opera House. The center section of seats was left unprotected from the elements. This concept was highly acclaimed except by the unfortunate customers who had seats in the uncovered portion on rainy nights. After one such experience, opera-goers quickly learned to check their ticket locations before parting with their money.

Kelsey remembered the year before when she had spent an entire evening huddled under a sheet of plastic to see *Eugene Onegin*. The rain had dripped down, but Brent had laughed and pulled her comfortably against him, saying that he'd have to wring her out before he let her in the car afterward. Kelsey drew in her breath sharply, remembering how pleasantly those lean hands of his had managed that interlude.

"Oh, damn!" she said unhappily, and steadied her lips as she turned into the big parking lot opposite the Opera House's main entrance. Daisy stirred impatiently on the front seat as Kelsey braked and cut the ignition. "Not this time, girl," Kelsey told her, reaching for the manila envelope of proofs which was between them. Daisy whined as Kelsey checked her lipstick in the visor mirror. "You can't go," Kelsey said, buttoning her jacket and putting the car keys in the pocket. "If the security guards here didn't throw you out—Norman certainly would. That's what happens when you vacuum your whiskers with a man's trousers. I'll roll the window down so you'll have plenty of air," she said, suiting her actions to her words before getting out and closing the door. Daisy whined again but fortunately didn't start barking.

Kelsey hoped to slip quietly into the big outdoor theater, deliver the envelope to Norman, and go on her way. It would take extra time to explain her mission to the Opera House security people on duty, although she was sure they wouldn't object. Fortunately, there wasn't anyone around the shuttered gift section or the ticket windows by the entrance gates when she approached. Most of the gates were locked but she finally found the end one ajar and pushed through it. The metal squeaked as she shoved the gate back the way she'd found it and the sound seemed to slice through the quiet night air. Until that moment, she hadn't noticed that the rain had abated and even the breeze had died—there wasn't a leaf stirring on the shrubbery along the walk.

Then suddenly the chords of a rehearsal piano filtered up from the stage area and Kelsey recognized the lilting "O Paradiso" aria from Meyerbeer's *L'Africaine*. Evidently a tenor was in residence, showing that another of the benefit performers was changing his program.

That would really put the finishing touch to Norman's mood, Kelsey thought as she went down the outside steps at the left side of the building, taking care to stay in the shadows as she headed for the stage door.

There was only a glow from the stage area to her right, but that, combined with the disembodied strains of music floating through the still air, made the scene as unreal as any of the operatic plots unveiled during the season.

So far as Kelsey was concerned, it was an atmosphere that could have been skipped. She shivered as she scurried past a deserted refreshment stand where she'd lingered and drunk coffee in happier times. At that moment its shuttered outlines were clear, but even as she watched, the moon slipped into the thick storm clouds and finally disappeared—causing murky darkness to shroud the patio again. When the light disappeared, a sharp protesting bark came from Daisy in the parking lot, and as if triggered by a cue from some stage director, rain started falling steadily.

"Oh, great—just what I needed," Kelsey muttered, moving as fast as her ankle would allow toward the nearest door.

Fortunately, it was unlocked and apparently led into the subterranean storage area below the big stage where costumes were housed as well as scenery for the opera company's wide range of productions.

Kelsey went through the costume section hesitantly, wishing that she'd set a more explicit meeting place with Norman. All she needed was to come face to face with a gung-ho security officer who'd take a dim view of her presence there. She made her way on to the wig shop and found that it was as deserted as the costume premises. Out in the dimly lit corridor beyond, she tried to remember the route of an earlier backstage tour she'd taken and decided that the scenery storage area would be the next logical place to try.

It was even less inviting than the costume sector because there was something gay and frivolous about satins and laces piled on tables, and there wasn't anything remotely cheerful about towering pieces of furniture stacked alongside scenery flats in a dimly illuminated cavernous room as big as a neighborhood super market. Kelsey half-turned to survey it and gasped at an unexpected figure which loomed in front of her. An instant later her shoulders sagged as she recognized her own dim outlines in a weathered mirror propped against a bedstead.

Only the murmur of a masculine voice in the distance kept her from giving up and retreating to the iron stairway which led to stage level. She took a deep breath and walked on, past neatly stacked sections of balconies and barred windows. Were they from *Tosca*, she wondered, or was it *Manon Lescaut*?

Some tenor or soprano was bound to be languishing behind them before long.

She didn't waste any time turning the corner and finally saw Norman's familiar figure slouched atop a table at the far wall. He was talking on a telephone with his back to her, so intent on his conversation that he apparently didn't hear her footsteps. The air took on a chill as she walked toward him—a puzzling circumstance which only became evident when she reached the end of the room.

"And you objected to meeting me in the parking lot," she accused as he put down the telephone receiver. "I don't see why—this is practically a loading dock."

Norman's glum expression didn't lighten at her words. "I don't know why *you're* complaining—I'm the one who's been freezing in this place."

"I'm surprised you didn't light a fire," she said, gesturing toward some fireplace facades piled nearby, complete with electric logs.

"Very funny. You might like to know that I've been working while I was waiting for you. Now I have a temperamental tenor who doesn't like the backdrop that's been chosen."

Kelsey put a hand to her head and closed her eyes dramatically. "Don't tell me—he's the one who wants to sing Meyerbeer instead of Puccini."

"How the hell do you know that?"

"The spirits tell all," she intoned before opening her eyes. "Besides, he was rehearsing when I came in. What happened to your baritone?"

"I told him I'd throttle him if he changed another note. Did you find any more mistakes on those proofs?" Norman asked, taking the manila envelope from her without ceremony.

"To be honest, I didn't have time to look."

"That's a help." He threw the envelope on the table in disgust. "At least you're honest about it. I'm sorry now that I ever got involved."

"I just didn't have time," she protested feebly. "What with my ankle and everything ..."

"What does your ankle have to do with my program? Not that you don't have very sexy ankles," he went on, favoring her with a theatrical leer. "I've always liked looking at them."

"Well, don't bother now. I zigged when I should have zagged in Brent's car this morning and came off second best. But at least a sprained ankle isn't serious."

Norman's frowning glance swept downward for the first time. "Give me that again, will you? What were you doing in his car in the first place?"

"Driving it, in the first place," she said flippantly. "It wasn't until the second place that I took a dive in the ditch. Courtesy of a severed brake cable or something like that. At least that's what the man at the garage said when Brent asked afterward." She limped over to inspect the loading dock nearby and then retraced her footsteps. "That's why I wasn't in when you called. Brent found me right after it happened and took me to the clinic."

Norman looked more shaken at the news than Kelsey had ever seen him. He grimaced remorsefully, putting an arm around her shoulders. "And here I am—browbeating you over a stupid proofreading job after all that. But what were you doing in Brent's station wagon when you have a perfectly good car of your own?"

"It's too complicated to explain." She patted his cheek to soften her words and took the opportunity to slip out from under his arm. "Anyhow, I can check those ad proofs with you now."

"Can't do it, love. I'll have to take them with me." He straightened and ran a finger around his neck, as if his shirt collar was too tight. "When I couldn't get in touch with you, I made another dinner date tonight. Actually, it's more than just a date . . ."

"You don't have to explain," Kelsey said emphatically. She had no intention of lingering in the cold loading area any longer than she had to—especially to hear his confession about Geraldine's new-found attraction. He was due to be disappointed on that score but she didn't want to be around when the reckoning came. "This is the strangest place," she said to change the subject, and moved over to where a rope barrier cordoned off an abrupt drop into a black abyss. "Good Lord, it must be twenty feet to the bottom. You could lose a whole Wagnerian chorus down there. I don't remember seeing it when I toured this section before."

"That's because the elevator was probably at floor level then. It's a movable platform for scenery changes—similar to those in aircraft carriers. I wouldn't get too near that edge if I were you."

"Don't worry." She shuddered visibly and moved back toward him. "Talk about a hazard!"

"Maybe I should use it as an enforcer, if that tenor gives me any more trouble."

"Don't even joke about it." She pulled the lapels of her jacket together against the chilly air whistling through from the loading dock. "Well, I'm going if you don't need me for anything else. I still have a lot of packing to do."

Norman's head came up sharply. "Surely you weren't serious about leaving? You didn't let Brent talk you into anything, did you?"

"He doesn't have anything to do with it. At the moment he's busy working another side of the street. Don't you believe it about men preferring blondes—" Kelsey broke off as she saw the dark anger in Norman's face.

"If you're dropping hints about Geraldine, you've got it all wrong. When I told you that she was quitting her job, I just meant that she had another one in mind."

"Exactly. And I'm backing out so she can have a clear field," Kelsey said, tired of being a diplomat when nobody else was playing by the same rules. "I wouldn't wait dinner too long if I were you, because she's going to be a little late tonight. If she comes at all."

Norman's hand shot out like a talon, clamping onto her wrist painfully. "I told you to drop the innuendos."

Kelsey yanked her wrist away, furious with his action and yet amazed that he could have been so swayed by his sudden infatuation. "I wasn't being catty. Geraldine and Brent were together in the bar at El Torero when I left about an hour ago. I know for a fact that Brent had made dinner reservations."

Norman's freckled face paled. "She was with Brent? You're sure?"

"Very sure." Kelsey's voice was without emphasis but there was no doubting her sincerity. "She even had her arms around his neck. And I'm not any happier about it than you are."

Norman didn't appear to have even heard her. "She promised," he said, as if trying to convince himself. "She promised me faithfully just this morning that he didn't mean anything to her."

Kelsey stared at his brooding, dejected face and wished suddenly that she was anywhere but where she was at that moment. She took a step back, trying to make her movement casual. "Maybe I have it all wrong. They could have been discussing business."

"What kind? She doesn't work for him anymore. Why, she doesn't even know the reason he came back early from his European trip." Norman abruptly turned to stare at Kelsey, his expression malevolent. "You're the one with all the answers now."

Kelsey opened her lips to tell how little she knew and then closed them again as she remembered Brent's warning. "Not really. Nobody tells me anything." She tried to make a joke of it.

"You said that he was asking questions of the garage man," Norman accused.

"Well, wouldn't you if your brakes went out? I was a little curious myself."

"How could some high school kid who drives a tow truck give any information?" Norman scoffed. "Brent was just playing the big man again."

"He must have learned something," Kelsey shot back in defense. "Otherwise they wouldn't have a line on that fellow who works at Pecos. The one driving the van this afternoon."

Norman was visibly shaken but he rallied almost instantly. "It all sounds like a lot of mumbo-jumbo to me. Even if they question him, they won't learn anything. I'm sure of that."

His bluster made Kelsey do a double take. It was so foreign to what she'd thought he'd say. Just as if he knew all about the man at the Pecos Monument before she even mentioned him. Which was impossible unless . . . As her thoughts raced on, she took another step away from Norman, stumbling momentarily over some gilt chairs from a *Traviata* production.

Norman followed her, an almost pitying expression on his face. "You're so transparent, Kelsey. Right now, with that wide-eyed look you could be six years old—full of childish outrage because somebody smashed your favorite doll."

"My God," she exclaimed in horror. "Is that all it means to you? All these months—pretending to be my friend!" As the full implication hit her, she went on disbelievingly. "And Russ, did you let him down the same way? Maybe you even hired that mechanic to work on *his* car after Russ did the dirty work for you and Geraldine!"

"Leave her out of it," he snarled. "It's too bad you've been so damned curious, Kelsey. You don't leave me any choice now."

Norman was advancing steadily, keeping the gap between them small enough so that Kelsey couldn't dart around him and escape to the stair or the back loading dock. That only left the cordoned-off area

168

behind her where the elevator platform was at sub-basement level.

Even as that reality registered, Norman reached over to flick a wall switch, extinguishing the lights on the outside loading dock, and leaving only two bulbs overhead to penetrate the gloom. "I had a feeling this might be a good place to meet you, Kelsey, love. It's an instinct about people—I feel it when they turn against me. You were on Brent's side all along."

"And Russ's. That made it easy for you, didn't it?"

"Well, your stepbrother did have a regrettable single-mindedness. He tried to change his mind in the middle, you see. That didn't leave me any alternative." As Norman saw her sag under the impact of his words, his thin features hardened. "We've talked enough. I'm sorry but there's no other way, Kelsey." He jerked his head toward the concrete drop-off even as he closed the distance between them. "The stage crew will find you in the morning."

"You won't get away with anything here." She had to swallow before the words would come out.

"Of course I will," he replied, sounding disconcertingly confident. "The plot's simple; I planned to meet you backstage later tonight. Unfortunately, you suffered this tragic accident while I was still up there, trying to convince that tenor to stay on key. It never occurred to me to look for you in this part of the building." He took another step toward her and Kelsey, in trying to stay out of his reach, felt the cord that roped off the drop pressing into her back—leaving her a foot and a half of safety at the most, she reasoned frantically. She took a shuddering breath, her lungs rasping with the effort.

Even as she wondered what to do next, she knew with a horrible fatalism that Norman's plan could work. There would be suspicion but there'd be nothing anyone could prove. No evidence to tamper with this time. Just a closed folder in a metal file.

If she'd only waited for Brent to come with her—not been such a jealous fool! It was the story of her life, she thought despairingly—too much love and not enough faith.

Kelsey clutched the cord behind her as she realized she couldn't retreat any further. Well, she might go over the edge, but damned if she'd make it easy for him! Norman was going to have a fight on his hands—every inch of the way!

He must have realized it because his thin, almost womanish hands clenched and his expression was murderous as he started to close in.

They were both so intent that neither heard the newcomer until Daisy's powerful bulk suddenly lunged between them, coming up against Norman before he could protect himself.

He was off-balance to start with and Kelsey stood stricken as he tried to regain his footing on the edge of the concrete. When his hand clutched her shoulder, pulling her down with him, she started to scream. Her knees gave way, and all she could see in front of her was the yawning black cavity beneath.

Chapter 8

EVERYTHING blurred mercifully after that.

Kelsey *was* conscious of noise—staccato barks and a screaming that never seemed to stop. There were heavy masculine voices and one that sounded shrill in the cavernlike room. The screaming was finally replaced with a sobbing which might have gone on forever if someone hadn't put a cold wet rag on her face. At the same time, a familiar voice was saying, "Try to get hold of yourself, darling. It's over—you're all right."

She hiccuped but managed to steady her breathing, finally opening her eyes as the firm words penetrated. "Brent!" she said, finding it a relief to get the word out.

"I'm right here. I've come to take you home."

They were the nicest words she'd ever heard and she closed her eyes again, relaxing in his protective clasp. Her eyelids stayed down until the wet rag was put against her cheek once more, then she protested weakly. "Take it away, I don't need it."

"Maybe not now," Brent said roughly, "but Daisy was worth her weight in gold five minutes ago."

"Daisy?" Kelsey's lashes fluttered upward again.

This time she became aware that she was slumped in a chair out by the loading dock and that the wet rag was in reality Daisy's tongue, enthusiastically applied at random as she bounced around them.

"If you feel up to it, I'll carry you to the car—" Brent began, only to break off when Kelsey clutched his arm. "What's the matter?"

"Norman! What happened to him?"

"Not much." Brent's tone was laconic. "We got there in time to pull him back from the edge, too. Right now, he's in custody and on his way to jail. You missed most of the excitement."

Her eyes were dark with pain as they stared up at him. "Not enough. He's to blame for everything, Brent. All these months when he pretended to be Russ's friend—he was in that mess with him."

Brent shook his head. "You still haven't got it quite straight. Let's get out of this place and into some bright lights before the explanations start." He put his arm around her and helped her to her feet. "Can you manage or shall I carry you?"

"I'll be all right." She looked around, surprised to find they had the place to themselves. "Weren't there some other people here?"

His shoulders shook with amusement. "You bet there were! I picked up a couple local policemen on the way from town and they're going to notify federal authorities once Norman's behind bars. There'll be so many charges when they get them all together that he'll have to hire a team of lawyers. Even then, I don't think he'll get off the hook." Brent steered her toward the loading dock as he spoke. "Let's walk outside the building and go around the parking lot—

172

that way you won't have to negotiate those steep stairs. And the rain's stopped for the moment."

"What about Daisy?" Kelsey said, feeling much better once they got in the air. "She doesn't have a leash."

Brent chuckled again. "Take a look at her—she's dogging your heels." As Kelsey groaned at the pun, he apologized. "Sorry, I forgot you were in a weakened condition. Anyhow, since Daisy practically broke her neck to get to you, she won't wander off now."

"How did she get out of the car in the first place?"

"She was raising such a commotion when we parked alongside that I thought she'd break the window, so I let her out. Fortunately, you'd left me with a car key, even though you made off with the wheels."

His tone was matter-of-fact but Kelsey didn't hesitate to try and explain. "I'm sorry, Brent—I saw Geraldine in your arms at the bar in that restaurant . . ."

". . . so you put one and one together and came up with all the wrong answers again." His arm tightened momentarily around her shoulders. "We'll discuss that later, too."

Kelsey almost stumbled at his offhand reaction. She knew very well that if he'd left her stranded in the same way that she'd still be sticking pins in his effigy. Maybe he simply didn't care enough to object. But if that was so, why had he bothered to follow her to the Opera House?

"You're at it again," Brent's dry tone sounded next to her ear. "Why don't you take the rest of the night off or at least give me the benefit of the doubt? Daisy, get away from there!" The last came as the Airedale detoured by a refreshment stand where a discarded candy wrapper fluttered in the breeze. Brent frowned and addressed Kelsey. "Didn't she eat tonight?"

Kelsey started to laugh, despite herself. At that moment, his impatient question was the burst of normalcy that she needed to put life in the proper perspective. All the things she'd feared and worried about were in the past. Brent and the Airedale loping beside her represented the present. If the fates were bountiful—they might even be in her future. "Daisy had dinner—but I didn't. And I'm starving," she informed him. She reached down to clutch the dog's collar when they drew up beside the car at the edge of the parking lot.

"Serves you right." Brent unlocked the car door and snapped his fingers for the dog to bound onto the rear seat before standing back so that Kelsey could slide in the front. "Next time you'll stick around for a Margarita before you run off."

She waited until he'd closed the door and gone around to get in behind the steering wheel before saying ruefully, "I deserved that, I suppose . . ." and looked up in surprise when Brent gave a burst of laughter.

"Don't worry, you can have a crust of bread later." He settled his shoulders against the car door and remained facing her. "We might as well get the discussion over now. All right with you?"

"Yes, of course." Kelsey eased her aching ankle by

174

stretching it in front of her. The comfort and warmth of the car seemed wonderful after what had happened in the Opera House. Through the half-opened window beside her, she heard the last strains of "O Paradiso" and realized with surprise that the tenor was still rehearsing on stage.

Brent acknowledged it with a jerk of his head. "At least we have a pleasant background. Try to remember that."

"Instead of Norman? And Russ?"

"You don't have to be ashamed of that stepbrother of yours," Brent said, his voice deep. "Keeping that news quiet has been the hardest part of this whole thing."

"I don't understand . . ."

"Russ incriminated Norman at the outset of this mess. He wasn't sure of his facts—just that Norman promised him a big payoff for some of the stuff we were working on at the time. The offer was pretty nebulous and Russ didn't have any concrete evidence. In fact, he was hesitant about mentioning it to me at all. He *did* promise to let me know if anything developed."

"And did he?" she asked eagerly, unable to keep quiet any longer.

"The next thing I knew he was dead—killed in that car accident after leaving the building where the theft occurred."

"But why didn't you tell me about all this?" she wailed. "All these months of thinking he was a thief—"

"Unfortunately, he was," Brent cut in. "And I

175

couldn't mention any of those extenuating circumstances because I was ordered not to. The authorities decided not to let anything interfere with their pursuit of Norman; any breath of suspicion and he would have backed off. Which would have meant that Russ had really died in vain." Brent paused before going on distinctly. "We had to keep all avenues open. That included Geraldine."

"You mean *she* knew?"

"Not that we were suspicious. You see, Norman covered all bases—he tried to get Russ as an inside man in the beginning. Afterward, he set about cultivating Geraldine for another entree."

"I thought she was only interested in you," Kelsey said baldly. "That's what it looked like from my side of the fence."

"Geraldine's much like Norman—she believes in having plenty of strings to her bow at all times. I was told not to turn her off because she might prove valuable later."

Kelsey was stricken to hear that the suspicions she'd harbored so long were really true. "You mean that you—and Geraldine—really were . . ."

"Sleeping together?" His voice was grim. "If you hadn't had such a rough time already, I'd sure as hell put you over my knee for that."

"But you said . . ."

". . . that I was ordered to be nice to her. And I was. Nice, polite, considerate, an appreciative boss—but that's as far as it went. If you'll remember, I had another commitment at the time." Brent took a deep breath. "Let me get on with this, will you?

If we go off on tangents, we won't be out of this place by morning."

Kelsey was so overwhelmed by the flood of relief flowing over her that she would have agreed to practically anything. She sat back, saying happily, "I'm sorry. What happened next?"

"As we hoped, Norman tried to go too far and too fast with Geraldine. She wasn't against plenty of money in her future but she wanted to be around to enjoy it. Norman needed her help to get more classified information and promised that they'd get married right after he disposed of it to his contact. Geraldine had her suspicions about what happened to Russ and wasn't keen to follow through." Brent rubbed the back of his neck reflectively. "She sent word that she wanted to talk to me. Geraldine's a great one for taking care of number one."

"Did she have any proof about what happened to my brother?"

Brent shook his head. "But from the way Norman was babbling as they led him out tonight, it probably won't be necessary. Don't worry, honey—Russ's name will be completely cleared before it's over."

"But you said that he *did* take the material . . ."

"That's right. What we *didn't* reveal was that the data was agreed on beforehand. It was classified but not especially valuable—nor were the figures strictly accurate."

"But Norman didn't know that?"

"Nope. He swallowed the bait but slipped off the hook. Probably he met Russ on the road afterward. We don't know what caused the accident."

"Could that mechanic have been involved?"

"We'll sure as hell find out! Confession's good for the soul—and plea bargaining isn't unheard of."

"It's hard to understand how anybody could do such despicable things."

"Despicable but human. Norman wanted me out of the picture—both officially and every other way. God knows what Geraldine fabricated, but she probably told him that I was panting for her beautiful body from a distance."

Kelsey let her finger trail suggestively down his arm. "Just one thing . . ."

"What's that?"

"Make sure that it stays at a distance."

"Yes, ma'am." He nodded solemnly. "I always have."

"It didn't look like it at that restaurant tonight when she was hanging around your neck."

Brent stared at her puzzled. "I fended her off the only time she started clinging."

"Well, when I looked in, she was puckered up—and she wasn't kissing you good-bye," Kelsey said, giving a concise if inelegant report.

"If you'd looked a little longer, you'd have seen that she didn't kiss me at all. She was feeling sorry for herself and wanted sympathy."

"What did you do?"

"Told her to pull herself together," Brent said briskly and then grinned sheepishly when Kelsey dissolved with laughter. "Well, I was hungry and tired of waiting for you to appear. Afterward, when I found that you'd run out on me again I—"

"Would have beaten me if you'd had the chance," Kelsey said, before he could finish. "I'm just glad that you didn't give up on me completely. How did you ever find me here?"

"Vera. She called me back as soon as you'd left the house. After that, I rounded up reinforcements and came running. Thank God, Daisy took out after you like a shot, once I let her out of the car."

His somber words brought back that awful confrontation in the basement of the Opera House and Kelsey relived what might have happened to her if help hadn't arrived when it did.

She took a deep, calming breath and pushed the ghastly horror into oblivion. She had survived, it was over, and she'd never stop being grateful. But now there were other things to do.

"I suppose we'd better go to the police station and make a statement," she said, and sat up straight in the seat to show Brent that she was all right. "I'm starving but I can eat later. We should do the important things first."

"Exactly. But there's only one important thing now as far as I'm concerned." Brent's voice matched hers for briskness as he shifted on the car seat and bent toward her. "We'll take care of it now," he said, sliding his fingers in the neckline of her blouse and fastening on the gold chain. He'd unhooked it in a minute, carefully sliding off the ring before reaching for her left hand. "This goes back where it belongs," he said, putting the beautiful emerald-cut diamond on her finger.

"Now, for the rest of the schedule," he announced

in a tone of satisfaction. "After we take the dog back to Vera, we drive to Albuquerque and catch the first flight out for Nevada. That's so we can be married right away. I'm not taking any more chances on losing you." There was an expression on his face that she'd never seen before as he confessed, "I don't plan on letting you more than an arm's length from me until the honeymoon's over. That should take care of the first twenty years or so. After that, I'll let you make a few decisions."

Kelsey's heart was thumping so hard that she was sure it could be heard down on the stage of the Opera House and it was an effort to keep her voice steady. "Just a few of the decisions? This sounds more like a stock takeover than a proposal. You're being awfully businesslike."

"Only because if I get you in my arms—we'd be here all night." His glance was anything but businesslike as it swept over her. "There are other places for what I have in mind, my love."

"It's been so long since you called me that," she said tremulously. "I thought I'd never hear it again."

"You'll be hearing it for the rest of our lives." His voice was deep and none too steady either. "I've been waiting for such a long time—will you come with me now?"

Kelsey drew a breath and let it out blissfully. There were still things to explain, questions to ask. And she would, later on. But for now, one word really covered it all.

"Yes," she said. And then, so he couldn't possibly misunderstand, "Oh, darling—yes, please."

It should be confessed that neither Brent nor Kelsey found time for those serious discussions until considerable time had passed. Certainly there weren't any questions asked during their whirlwind trip to Las Vegas where Kelsey's engagement ring was removed again, but just long enough to be joined by a slender platinum wedding band.

After that, there was a brief honeymoon detour to Scottsdale where it's doubtful if either of them even knew what day it was, indicating their deplorable state of mind. It took until the following week when they were settled back in Santa Fe before they surfaced to reality. Vera saw that they were adequately fed but was tactful enough to leave the house promptly after dinner.

Even Daisy had adopted a "live and let live" policy. She had approved the removal of her bed to the guest room and took to it in the shank of the evening, thereby insuring that she wouldn't be late to breakfast.

Kelsey and Brent also adopted the latter practice though not with such commendable motives.

It was while they were getting ready for bed one night soon after their return that Kelsey brought up Daisy's former existence. "Now that you're safely in my clutches, I want the truth," she said to Brent, clad only in pajama bottoms, as he stood emptying change from his trouser pockets onto the top of his dresser. "Were those kennel people in England really going to destroy such a beautiful dog?"

Brent added a bunch of keys to the coins. "Maybe it wasn't that drastic. She *was* mixed up and she didn't get along with the male in the same run. In short, she reminded me of you," he finished, grinning.

"Well, I like that," Kelsey said in pretended indignation.

He came across the room and bent to where she sat on the edge of the bed, dropping a light kiss in the vicinity of her ear. "So do I—very much. When are you going to get ready for bed?"

She obediently got to her feet and started to unhook the gold chain at her neck.

"I'll help you with that," he said and took the clasp from her fingers. After it parted, he put his lips to her soft skin for an instant before pushing her determinedly away. "I should know better by now. Keep your distance, woman!"

Kelsey blew him a kiss and wandered over to her jewel box, saying, "Going back to Daisy—it's a good thing that I was still here to play kennel maid when you arrived. The poor dog would have gotten short shrift with Geraldine."

"There was never any chance of Daisy landing in her clutches," Brent said smugly. "You were set up, my girl. I kept damned close track of you, even on the other side of the country. I was only giving you a chance to cool off before I came back on the scene. Thank God, Norman finally started playing into our hands to make it easier, but I'd already served notice with Lucius and the rest of officialdom that you were the most important thing in my life. If Norman hadn't made his move then, I was still going to level with you."

"I'm glad," she said simply. "I couldn't have stood it alone much longer. But you looked so surprised when you arrived that morning—and there was all that mumbo-jumbo about needing me to look after Daisy."

"Well, I could hardly convince you to stay in the house without an excuse," Brent said, tossing his discarded shirt into a hamper. "I'd remembered that you were partial to Airedales, so Daisy fit into the scheme of things nicely."

"You Machiavelli." Kelsey pulled a peignoir of ivory lace from a hanger and draped it over her arm. "You had me completely fooled. I thought you couldn't stand the sight of me."

"It was either that or grabbing you by the hair and running off to the nearest justice of the peace. You needed some convincing before I managed that. And after the accident with the car, I was wishing I'd made you leave town to keep you safe."

Kelsey put a soft hand up to his cheek as she passed him on the way to her dressing table. "I thought so. What about your acting like a tyrant at our picnic and your 'therapy' afterward?"

Brent grinned, unabashed. "It's a good thing those school buses didn't arrive about five minutes later. My therapy had gotten completely out of hand—" He broke off as she cocked an inquisitive head. "What's the matter?"

"I thought I heard something." She sat in front

of the dressing table, a hairbrush immobile in her hand. "Did you lock the utility room door?"

"I'll double check and make sure. The last thing we need is company." He dropped a swift kiss on the top of her head en route. "Don't go away."

It wasn't long before he was back again, his shoulders shaking with laughter. Kelsey looked quizzically across at him as she got into bed.

"Was I imagining things?" she asked. "Or was it Daisy?"

"Daisy's sound asleep in the guest bedroom, stretched out on the rug." As Kelsey raised an eyebrow, Brent's grin broadened. "I forgot to mention that Elmo is also sound asleep—in the middle of the dog bed."

"The fiend," she said resignedly. "So be it. I wonder what I heard."

"It might have been a rustling in the utility room." Brent raked a hand through his hair as he came over beside her. "You know that fixture over the laundry tray? That fool mouse of yours was curled up in it, making a meal by nibbling on the bar of soap."

"I only hope Vincent has the good sense to leave before morning. Otherwise I'll have to throw him out again before Elmo wakes up." She paused as he leisurely got into bed and pushed back the covers. "Darling—whatever are you doing?"

"Following Vincent's plan, with a few modifications, of course." He pulled her close beside him. "And you'll find me much harder to get rid of."

"Brent, you can't . . ."

There was a smothered burst of laughter from her.

Later, a deep chuckle and a murmured endearment from him.

Considerably later, a sigh of satisfaction from them both.

And finally, the light went out.

ABOUT THE AUTHOR

Glenna Finley is a native of Washington State. She earned her degree from Stanford University in Russian Studies and in Speech and Dramatic Arts, with emphasis on radio.

After a stint in radio and publicity work in Seattle, she went to New York City to work for NBC as a producer in its international division. In addition, she worked with the "March of Time" and *Life* magazine.

As a producer, she had her own show about activities in Manhattan, a show that was broadcast to England. The programs were similar to those of the "Voice of America."

Though her life in New York was exciting, she eventually returned to the Northwest where she married. Currently residing in Seattle with her husband, Donald Witte, and their son, she loves to travel, and draws heavily on her travels and experiences for the novels that have been published. Her books for NAL have sold several million copies.